Allen Rodol

A boy who became the strongest swordsman in the land after pressing the 100-Million-Year Button. For reasons unknown, he is invited to the New Year's Jubilee, an event hosted by the empress of Liengard.

CONTENTS

CHAPTER 1
The Transfer Student & Christmas
001

CHAPTER 2
An Invitation & a Demon
065

CHAPTER 3
The Allen Cell & a Political Marriage
119

Afterword
169

I KEPT PRESSING THE 100-MILLION-YEAR BUTTON AND CAME OUT ON TOP
~THE UNBEATABLE REJECT SWORDSMAN~ 6

SYUICHI TSUKISHIMA

Illustration by MOKYU

New York

I KEPT PRESSING THE 100-MILLION-YEAR BUTTON AND CAME OUT
ON TOP: ~THE UNBEATABLE REJECT SWORDSMAN~
SYUICHI TSUKISHIMA

Translation by Luke Hutton
Cover art by Mokyu

This book is a work of fiction. Names, characters, places, and incidents are the product
of the author's imagination or are used fictitiously. Any resemblance to actual events,
locales, or persons, living or dead, is coincidental.

1 OKUNEN BUTTON WO RENDA SHITA ORE HA, KIZUITARA SAIKYO NI
NATTE ITA Vol.6 ~RAKUDAI KENSHI NO GAKUIN MUSO~
©Syuichi Tsukishima, Mokyu 2021
First published in Japan in 2021 by KADOKAWA CORPORATION, Tokyo.
English translation rights arranged with KADOKAWA CORPORATION, Tokyo,
through TUTTLE-MORI AGENCY, INC., Tokyo

English translation © 2023 by Yen Press, LLC

Yen Press, LLC supports the right to free expression and the value of copyright.
The purpose of copyright is to encourage writers and artists to produce the creative
works that enrich our culture.

The scanning, uploading, and distribution of this book without permission is a theft
of the author's intellectual property. If you would like permission to use material from
the book (other than for review purposes), please contact the publisher. Thank you for
your support of the author's rights.

Yen On
150 West 30th Street, 19th Floor
New York, NY 10001

Visit us at yenpress.com
facebook.com/yenpress
twitter.com/yenpress
yenpress.tumblr.com
instagram.com/yenpress

First Yen On Edition: October 2023
Edited by Yen On Editorial: Maya Deutsch
Designed by Yen Press Design: Andy Swist

Yen On is an imprint of Yen Press, LLC.
The Yen On name and logo are trademarks of Yen Press, LLC.

The publisher is not responsible for websites (or their content) that are not owned by
the publisher.

Library of Congress Cataloging-in-Publication Data
Names: Tsukishima, Syuichi, author. | Mokyu, illustrator. | Hutton, Luke, translator.
Title: I kept pressing the 100-million-year button and came out on top /
Syuichi Tsukishima ; illustration by Mokyu ; translation by Luke Hutton.
Other titles: Ichiokunen button o renda shita ore wa, kizuitara saikyo ni natte ita. English
Description: First Yen On edition. | New York, NY : Yen On, 2021–
Identifiers: LCCN 2021034588 | ISBN 9781975322342 (v. 1 ; trade paperback) |
ISBN 9781975322366 (v. 2 ; trade paperback) | ISBN 9781975322380
(v. 3 ; trade paperback) | ISBN 9781975343163 (v. 4 ; trade paperback) |
ISBN 9781975343187 (v. 5 ; trade paperback) | ISBN 9781975343200
(v. 6 ; trade paperback)
Subjects: LCGFT: Fantasy fiction. | Light novels.
Classification: LCC PL876.S857 I3413 2021 | DDC 895.6/36—dc23
LC record available at https://lccn.loc.gov/2021034588

ISBNs: 978-1-9753-4320-0 (paperback)
978-1-9753-4321-7 (ebook)

10 9 8 7 6 5 4 3 2 1

LSC-C

Printed in the United States of America

CHAPTER 1

The Transfer Student & Christmas

The first thing Claude did after transferring abruptly to Thousand Blade Academy was call me "maggot." Evidently, her animosity toward me had only grown over the half year since we'd last seen each other. My classmates all began to speak at once as I tried to figure out how best to respond.

"Chairwoman Reia said she was a 'beautiful swordswoman,' right? So why's she wearing a guy's uniform?" a male student wondered aloud.

"She's a pretty girl who dresses like a boy... *Ahhh*, that's so cool!" squealed one of my female classmates. Claude must've been the type to be popular with the same gender.

Chairwoman Reia cleared her throat to quiet the class.

"As I said, Claude is an elite swordswoman from the prestigious Royal Vesteria Academy. Her finely honed swordcraft skills should be an inspiration for you all. I suggest you work together with her to make the most out of your limited school time," she said before pointing behind me. "Claude, I've placed you at the desk behind Allen. Please take a seat."

Of course the chairwoman found the worst possible spot to put her.

"Hmph… that works for me," Claude said with a malicious grin. She walked across the room and sat in the spot behind me.

I can feel her eyes boring a hole through the back of my skull… I could tell she was staring at me without even needing to turn around.

"Claude! What are you doing at Thousand Blade?!" Lia exclaimed once the class had settled down. Why *had* Claude come all the way from Vesteria to join this Liengardian school? I was as eager to find out as Lia.

Does she know about the recent incident? A few months ago, Lia had been abducted by two members of the Black Organization, Zach Bombard and Tor Sammons. We succeeded in rescuing her thanks to a tip-off from Rize Dorhein, but I had expected that Vesteria would raise more of a fuss at their princess being kidnapped. Yet for some reason, the kingdom was strangely quiet about it.

Maybe King Vesteria only learned about what happened recently and is trying to drag Lia home. But if that was the case, it wouldn't make sense for him to have Claude transfer to Thousand Blade. She could've just come and fetched Lia without going through the trouble of becoming a student here. And Vesteria was one of the Five Powers—there was no way they were only just now learning about the abduction, months after it had happened.

The more I think about it, the less sense it makes… Why did Claude transfer to Thousand Blade? What's the king thinking? I pondered those questions as Claude answered hesitantly.

"I came…to check on your situation, Your Highness," she said.

"…?! H-huh… All right, then," Lia responded hastily, seeming satisfied.

Lia's "situation?" What does that mean? I wondered.

The chairwoman clapped her hands. "Okay, now that I've introduced Claude, let's move on to first period! We're doing basic strength training today with a focus on the lower body and stamina. Get ready to work up a sweat!"

My fellow Class 1-A students and I shuffled out of the classroom and headed to the schoolyard for first period.

■

We ended up spending the first two periods on intense strength training, rather than basic, and I took a huge stretch once we were done.

"Phew... I've always loved winter classes," I said. The chilly breeze felt incredible on my flushed body.

"Hmm-hmm, oh Allen... You love school all year round, not just during winter," Lia said with an amused grin.

"Ha, you really are a fitness freak," Rose teased.

"A-ha-ha, I won't deny it," I responded.

I feel like we've had this conversation before..., I thought. I started to head toward the classroom but was quickly interrupted.

"It's finally lunch time, maggot," Claude said, smiling cheerfully and grasping me by the shoulders.

"Yeah... And?" I asked. *This can't be good.*

"I thought this would be the perfect opportunity to teach you a lesson."

"...What do you mean?"

"Must I spell everything out...? I'm getting revenge for our last match—right here, right now!"

She whipped her sword out of its sheath and pointed it at me.

"*Haah...*," I sighed. I'd suspected she might try to pull this, but couldn't she have at least waited until the end of the day? Talk about being impatient.

"Is that new girl serious?! She just picked a fight with Allen on her first day!"

"Does she have a death wish?! That guy's practically invincible..."

"B-but, Claude goes to the top swordcraft academy in Vesteria! She might have a shot!"

Claude's challenge sent a wave of interest through my classmates.

...*Well, shoot.* I had no desire to fight in that moment. I definitely wanted to cross blades with her, but it was hardly the time. I needed to make it to my regular meeting with the Student Council that we held every lunch period. *I could skip the meeting... But then I'd have to watch Shii pout like a child. She'd be really upset.*

"Would you mind if we did this after sch—"

"Yes, I would," Claude interjected.

"I see..." She clearly wasn't going to let me wriggle out of this. "*Haah... Fine. Let's do it.*"

Seeing no alternative, I accepted Claude's challenge.

"Go easy on her, okay Allen? I don't want her getting hurt too badly," Lia requested, sounding seriously concerned for Claude.

"That might be difficult...," I responded. Claude was very skilled—I wouldn't be able to take her down without giving it my all.

"Excuse me, Your Highness?! Do you really think I'm going to lose to this maggot twice?!" Claude shouted in disbelief.

"Ah-ha-ha, it's nothing against you, Claude. Allen's just really strong," Lia said with an adorably apologetic grin.

"Y-you bastard... You've been poisoning her mind again! Is there no end to your lascivious ways?!" Claude glared at me accusatorily.

"Hey, can you not make me sound so sinister?!" I protested. I had enough baseless rumors to worry about already. My reputation would be tarnished even more if people got it in their heads that I'd deceived the princess of Vesteria.

"I challenge you to a duel, maggot!" Claude proclaimed.

"What?!" I shouted. I had expected a practice match. Duels were serious affairs between swordfighters with pride and stakes on the line.

"Whoever wins gets to give the loser a command they can't refuse!"

"...Just so you know, I won't follow any ridiculous orders like 'never interact with Lia again.'"

"Don't worry. My demand will be perfectly reasonable."

Apparently, she'd already decided what she was going to order me to do.

"Okay... I accept," I said.

"Ha, then we've got ourselves a duel! Draw Breath—Abio Troupe!" Claude shouted, smiling belligerently. She wasted no time summoning her Soul Attire.

I quickly drew my sword and assumed the middle stance. *It's been about half a year since I fought Claude. This will actually be a solid opportunity to see how much I've grown in that time.*

"Let's do this, Allen Rodol!"

"Give me your all!"

And so my duel with Claude began.

■

I held out my naked blade and matched Claude's gaze. *This is already going differently than last time.* She'd attacked as soon as the duel started when we fought in the Grand Coliseum. Now, however, she was watching me carefully.

I figured she would immediately leap at me, given her aggressive personality. I wonder if she's changed her fighting style, or if she has a certain strategy in mind this time?

Heavy beads of sweat formed on Claude's forehead as I considered the situation.

"Y-you've improved significantly in the short time since our last duel...," she admitted reluctantly.

"Do you think so? Thank you very much," I responded. I never thought I'd hear praise from her, of all people.

"He's far more skilled than I anticipated... I should avoid close combat," Claude muttered. Then she slashed the ground of the schoolyard three times with her longsword, forming a light-blue crest. The earth in front of her began to morph...

"*Tweet, tweet!*"

Chapter 1

"*Cawww!*"

"*Hoo, hoo!*"

...transforming into a swallow and a crow that were about the size of my fists, along with an owl the size of a barrel. The two smaller birds landed on Claude's shoulders, while the larger one flew high into the sky.

Here we go again. Claude's Soul Attire, Abio Troupe, had the formidable ability to transform inorganic matter into bombs that she could freely manipulate. It had given me a lot of trouble six months back.

"Hah, you're in for a world of pain if you think this is going to play out like last time," Claude threatened smugly before swinging her longsword.

"*Tweet, tweet!*"

The swallow flew gracefully from her shoulder, landed on a spot where no one was standing, and exploded with a deafening *boom*. The smoke and dust cleared to reveal a giant crater in the ground.

"Huh?!" I gasped.

That blast was as strong as the ones her owls had produced during our last duel. *Her bombs have gotten way more powerful... I need to watch out for that owl.* I looked up at the giant raptor while keeping Claude in the corner of my vision. If the tiny swallows contained that much explosive force, there was no telling how big the owl's detonation would be.

"Ha-ha, did that catch you off guard?" Claude taunted.

"Sure did. I can't believe that tiny swallow packed that big of a punch... You've gotten a lot stronger in the last six months," I said.

"Of course I have. I've been putting myself through hellish training day after day ever since losing to you!"

Claude sliced the ground again.

""*Tweet, tweet!*"""

""*Caw! Caw!*"""

She created ten swallows and crows each, totaling twenty bombs. *The number of explosives she can produce has gone up... Her limit was around* ten last time, but now she can craft twenty at once. It's truly unbelievable how much she's grown.

"Have I shocked you speechless? You're not withstanding this blast! Now, *dance*, maggot!" Claude commanded, and the twenty bombs rushed toward me with astounding speed.

They're so fast...

The singing birds reached point-blank range before I had time to react.

"Detonate!" Claude commanded.

The explosives ignited in a terrific blast, blinding me with bright light. Silence fell upon the schoolyard once the echo faded, and a massive cloud of dust obscured the spot where I'd been standing.

"Hah, it worked!" Claude cheered, certain of her victory.

"Sh-should we be concerned? That looked pretty bad..."

"I'd be disintegrated by an explosion like that..."

"A-Allen... You're alive in there, right...?"

My classmates buzzed anxiously.

"Of course I am," I said, just before clearing the dust with my darkness to prove I was unharmed.

"Y-you cannot be serious..." Claude gasped, stepping back with a look of astonishment on her face.

"You really are special, Claude. Your strength, the number of bombs you can create, your speed—they're all on another level. But you're not the only one who's grown since our last duel," I said.

My cloak of darkness was way too durable for Abio Troupe's swallows and crows to break through. I bet I could take thousands of those explosions without being injured.

"There's *no way* you should be able to take a blast of that size and come out unscathed. What is that baleful power of yours?!" Claude asked, pointing at the darkness that cloaked my entire body.

"Oh yeah, you haven't seen this before," I responded. This hardly would've been a fair duel if I knew what she was capable of, but not the other way around. "I have the ability to summon and freely manipulate darkness, which can both strengthen my body and mend wounds. With this gloom at my command, I can protect people—and heal them to boot. It's a kind, gentle power."

"Don't tell me...did you manifest your Soul Attire?!"

"Yes. Only a few days ago, though. I'm still learning how to use it."

I ended the conversation there and summoned more darkness, which rose from my body to block the sunlight and cast a large shadow over the schoolyard.

"I guess it's my turn, then. Dark Shadow!" I yelled. I held my right hand forward, and an abyssal gloom crept across the schoolyard toward Claude.

That's weird, I thought. The nature of my darkness felt a little different than it had before I manifested my Soul Attire. There was a...menacing quality to it, just like Claude said. *Am I becoming more like* him?

First, I'd gotten stronger inexplicably, seemingly overnight. Then my hair suddenly turned black and white. And now, my darkness had turned wicked and foreboding. Slowly but surely, I was beginning to resemble my Spirit Core.

I have no idea if I should be excited or alarmed. I'll bring it up with Chairwoman Reia next time I see her, I thought.

"Not good enough!" Claude yelled. She jumped high in the air and ordered the owl to descend; the two essentially swapped places.

"Hoooooo!"

The owl then exploded, and the blast moved downward to deflect my approaching Dark Shadow.

So Claude can direct explosions now... Anyway, I was right to be wary of the owls. They're strong enough to deflect Dark Shadow with one blow. I doubted that even the cloak of darkness would be enough to completely neutralize an explosion of that magnitude.

"What happened to your excellent swordcraft, maggot? Don't hold back!" Claude shouted, glaring at me as she produced her next owl bomb. She seemed angry that I hadn't immediately followed up with another attack after firing Dark Shadow.

"Got it. Prepare yourself," I responded. I sheathed my blade and shifted my weight downward.

My cloak of darkness renders the swallows and crows ineffective. I just have to figure out how to deal with the owls. In our last duel, I won by throwing caution to the wind and charging straight into an explosion to catch her unawares, but she'll be ready for that this time. I might be able to withstand her explosion if I pull the same trick, but she would dodge my blow with a calm backstep.

I need to attack fast—so fast that Claude won't be able to react, and the owl won't be able to reach me. I don't know if I can pull that off, but it's worth trying!

I planted my feet firmly, then kicked off the ground...and found myself right in Claude's face before my brain even processed that I had moved.

"Wh-what?!" she gasped, eyes wide in shock at how quickly I had entered range for a deadly strike. "H-Hegemonic Style—Hard Strike!"

She swung her sword down at an angle, but I quickly dodged it and whirled behind her.

"Seventh Style—," I began.

"No! This isn't happening!" she screamed, twisting away desperately while keeping me in her sights.

I could learn from her indomitable spirit..., I thought, before unleashing my fastest skill. Doing anything less would be an insult to Claude.

"—Draw Flash!" I yelled, performing a slash that surpassed the speed of sound.

The speed of that move! Should I try to block it? No, that's impossible. It'll kill me if I don't dodge it..., Claude thought as the blade zipped toward her.

I stopped my sword right before it hit her neck.

"I win. Do you accept defeat?" I asked.

Chapter 1

"...Yes. You've bested me," Claude admitted reluctantly. She let Abio Troupe slip from her hands, signaling the end of the duel.

"Phew...," I sighed with relief. I had defeated Claude Stroganof.

"Good job, Allen. Your darkness felt different... Has it gotten more powerful?" Lia asked after rushing toward me.

"That was a fine bout... I swear you were faster than before," Rose said after joining her.

"I'm guessing that's a result of manifesting my Soul Attire...," I responded.

I had felt my Spirit Core's presence more intimately since manifesting Zeon. I used to have to concentrate to use the darkness, but now I could manipulate it as freely as my own arms and legs.

How should I classify my Soul Attire? That's a difficult question...

Its main ability was that of a simple self-strengthening Soul Attire, but it could also manipulate darkness like remote-control Soul Attire, and it even had the restorative powers of a rare healing Soul Attire. It was so versatile that I had trouble categorizing it.

"You damn maggot... How did you grow so much stronger in such a short amount of time?!" Claude demanded furiously, jabbing a finger at me.

"I don't know how to answer that... I didn't do anything special," I said bluntly. I had only gone through the same fundamental training as everyone else at Thousand Blade Academy.

"Don't lie to me! There's no way you could've obtained such overwhelming strength and keen swordcraft without some secret!"

"Hmm..."

Do I have a secret? There's only one thing I can think of...

"I do more practice swings than anyone else. I guess that could be the source of my improvement."

"P-practice swings...? I see you have no intention of sharing your method of training with me..."

"Huh..."

She seemed unconvinced by my answer. I was being completely honest, though...

"Forget about that for now, Claude. Are you going to honor the agreement you made before the duel?" Lia asked. She was referring to Claude's proposal that the loser would have to obey a single command from the winner.

"I'm so sorry, Your Highness..."

"Why are you apologizing to me?" Lia responded.

"Because I was too weak. I wasn't able to release you from that heinous agreement...," Claude said, gritting her teeth and bowing deeply.

What heinous agreement? Oh, that's what she's talking about. She must have been trying to end the master-and-servant relationship between me and Lia. *That totally slipped my mind... But agreements resulting from duels are absolute. I'm still technically Lia's master.*

"Y-you don't have to worry about that...," Lia muttered, blushing slightly and looking away.

"Don't tell me... Have you *accepted* this foul arrangement?!" Claude asked, going pale-faced and falling to her knees. I got the sense there had been a major misunderstanding.

"No, what's not what I... Anyway, enough about that! You should worry about yourself first!" Lia scolded. I walked over to Claude.

"Hmm... What should I ask you to do?" I wondered aloud, scratching my cheek.

"You animal..." Claude bristled. She covered her chest with her hands and retreated backward.

"I can give you any command, right?" I asked.

"Y-yes! I'll do anything you tell me to, so long as it's reasonable... Emphasis on reasonable!" she responded, blushing furiously.

Does she really see me as the kind of guy who would give her some lecherous command? She probably does, actually... Feeling a little hurt, I spoke candidly.

"I...don't really have anything I want to ask of you," I said.

"Huh?! You can give me any command you want! Surely a carnal beast like you must have something you'd like me to... What are you plotting?!" Claude demanded.

"I'm not a carnal beast, and I'm not plotting anything."

I had already gotten what I wanted out of this duel. My decisive victory was proof of how much I had grown over the last half a year. Pushing myself to swing my sword for hours on end every day had not been a waste of time. I was satisfied having learned that, so I couldn't think of anything I wanted to ask of her.

I could give her an inconsequential command to satisfy the agreement... But she'd probably just yell at me and say she doesn't need my pity. Given that, I decided it was best to just be honest.

"I don't have anything I want to order you to do right now," I repeated.

"Grk... Very well. It makes me sick to my stomach, but I'll let you keep this once-in-a-lifetime privilege in your back pocket. You'd *better* not forget about it," Claude warned.

"Uh, thank you...?"

I didn't think I would ever need to use it, but there was no reason not to take it. *Life is unpredictable. It could end up coming in handy in the future.* In Goza Village, we were taught not to waste food and to take what we were given. Surviving in a rural farming town like that was difficult without a tenacious spirit.

"I'm sure the president is waiting for us, so we should get moving," I said.

"Yeah, you're right," Lia agreed.

"Let's go," Rose responded.

"Huh? Did you say 'president'?" Claude asked, confused.

■

We dropped by Class 1-A to grab our lunches and went to the Student Council room. We could hardly leave Claude by herself in there on her first day, so we took her with us.

I know that we call them "meetings," but they're really just casual lunches. Bringing someone who's not on the Student Council shouldn't be a problem.

I knocked on the door to the Student Council room and entered with Lia, Rose, and Claude.

"You're late! Where the heck have you been?!" Shii fumed after storming toward me, visibly upset.

"C-can you please back up a bit, President?!" I asked, panicking. The scent of her pleasant shampoo tickled my nose, quickening my pulse.

"Tell me what you've been doing this whole time! Lunch started *twenty minutes ago!*" she yelled, puffing her cheeks. She liked to present herself as an older-sister type, but right now, she just came across as a spoiled child who hadn't gotten her way.

"Sorry, something came up," I responded awkwardly. Shii glared at me.

"Care to be more specific?"

"I had a duel with this student here. Her name is Claude."

"...Huh? You're Claude Stroganof, aren't you?"

Shii blinked in surprise. She seemed to know who Claude was.

"Yes, I am. I transferred here today from Royal Vesteria Academy. You must be Shii Arkstoria, Lilim Chorine, and Tirith Magdarote. Reia has told me of your prowess with the sword. I still have much to learn myself, but I hope we can share a fruitful school life here together," Claude said. She smiled softly and bowed. "These are Vesterian tea cakes. They're quite popular in my homeland. Please, help yourself."

"Wow, thank you very much," Shii responded.

"Ha, so Black Fist has recognized my strength... Soon the name Lilim Chorine will ring all throughout the land!" Lilim declared.

"Those look really good...," Tirith muttered, eyeing the Vesterian tea cakes.

Shii cleared her throat. "Welcome to the Student Council, Claude.

"A swordswoman of your caliber is always welcome! Would you be willing to join as a clerk?"

"Yes. It would be an honor," she responded.

That sure was quick. I wonder if Chairwoman Reia arranged for Claude to join the Student Council beforehand? I thought.

We quickly shared self-introductions and began eating lunch. Claude was quite affable, instantly breaking the ice with Rose, Shii, and even the slightly eccentric duo of Lilim and Tirith. At this rate, she would have no trouble fitting in with Class 1-A.

If only she could direct some of that kindness toward me..., I internally lamented as I ate the lunch Lia had made me.

"Oh yeah, you said you had a duel. Who won?" Shii asked after eating a sausage cut to look like an octopus.

"...I hate to admit it, but I was out of my league against Allen," Claude said with some effort.

Shii sighed loudly and glared at me. "*Haah...* There you go bullying girls for fun again, Allen."

"Can you please not make me sound so terrible...?" I responded.

"Hmm-hmm, sorry." Shii giggled like a mischievous child and turned to Claude. "Don't feel so bad about that. Allen can hardly even be considered human anymore. No one can beat him in a fair match."

"Don't let that gentle face of his fool you. He's a hot-blooded musclehead. Unless you cook up an ingenious scheme ahead of time, he's impossible to defeat," Lilim added.

"Jokes aside, he's brutally strong," Tirith said.

"That definitely matches my experience...," Claude admitted, clasping her chopsticks with regret. It looked like she was reflecting on our duel.

"Ah-ha-ha..." I laughed awkwardly, having no idea what to say.

We continued to enjoy our lunch, chatting about a variety of topics as we did so.

"The year is almost over," Lia muttered, staring off into the distance.

"Your Highness...," Claude said, dropping her gaze.

What was what? I wondered, curious about their behavior. I was about to ask her about it when Lia addressed me first.

"What did you think of this year, Allen?" she asked, her expression as bright as ever.

I thought she looked down for a moment there, but it must've been my imagination.

"Hmm... It had its challenges, but it was very fun," I replied.

Now that I thought about it, a whole lot had happened over the past year.

It all started with the 100-Million-Year Button. That unimaginable experience changed my life forever. Without it, I never would've been admitted to Thousand Blade and gotten to lead the hectic but fulfilling life I had now.

Since becoming a student here, I had fought in the Elite Five Holy Festival, spent a month working as a witchblade, enjoyed a summer training camp with Ice King Academy, competed in the First-Year Tourney and the Sword Master Festival, experienced the Thousand Blade Festival, and traveled abroad as a senior holy knight special trainee. And best of all, I'd met many incredible people along the way, including Lia, Rose, Claude, Shido, and Idora.

I can't decide if this year felt long or short... Either way, it sure was jam-packed with milestones.

"That reminds me. Have you all bought your presents yet?" Shii asked, holding up a finger.

"Huh? Presents?" I asked.

"Oh, do you not know about that yet?" Shii looked surprised.

"The official announcement is next week, Shii," Lilim said.

"The first-years haven't been told about it yet...," Tirith added.

"Oh yeah!" Shii clapped her hands excitedly and explained with a wide smile. "I'll fill you in now, I guess. Thousand Blade holds a Christmas party for the entire student body every year on December twenty-fifth!"

"Ooo, fun! What happens at the party?" Lia inquired enthusiastically.

"That sounds interesting," Rose remarked, also seeming excited.

"The entire student body gathers in the auditorium for a dinner party. There's also a gift exchange and famous musicians playing live music—it's a blast every year!" Shii said.

It sounded like a perfectly ordinary, if large-scale, Christmas party on the surface. But knowing Shii, I was a little worried...

"Make sure you come with empty stomachs! The food is cooked on-site by chefs from five-star restaurants!" Lilim exclaimed.

"It's a buffet, so you can stuff yourselves silly...," Tirith said.

"A buffet?!" Lia repeated excitedly, her eyes lighting up at the prospect of getting to eat as much as she wanted.

"The party sounds just as lavish as you'd expect from an Elite Five Academy," I said.

"Tee-hee, just wait until you see it. And that's not all—look forward to a little event at the end too," Shii hinted, giving her best wink and smile.

Oh, that's probably what has her so excited, I thought.

"And what exactly does *that* entail?" I asked.

"Tee-hee, you'll have to wait and see."

"Okay..."

I had spent enough time with Shii over the past year to tell what she was thinking by her smile. She had her sinister grins, her mischievous grins, and her spiteful grins. *Oh, that's weird... I don't have many positive memories associated with her smiling, do I? That smirk of hers means I'm very unlikely to enjoy whatever she's planning.*

I would need to steel myself for the Christmas "festivities".

"You're going to love it, I promise!" Shii reassured me.

"Details about the party will be shared soon. Don't forget to bring a present!" Lilim reminded us.

"And don't worry about helping with preparations. We'll take care of that ourselves…," Tirith added.

That was all the information they shared about the Christmas party.

■

The next few weeks were very fulfilling. I spent my days sharpening my swordcraft in class at Thousand Blade Academy, and my evenings working up a sweat with the Practice-Swing Club. My club had ballooned in size, and we'd just surpassed one hundred members, making us the second-largest student organization in the school after the Swordcraft Club. Now that my classmates knew the fun of practice swings, I was sure they would vote for my outdoor practice-swing meet at next year's Thousand Blade Festival.

I used my handful of days off to visit the Aurest branch of the Holy Knights Association and train with the senior holy knights.

"Are you sure about this?" Clown Jester had asked with a laugh the first time I showed up. "We can't teach you a thing."

Nonetheless, I was technically a senior holy knight special trainee. Considering that the program was designed to funnel people into the holy knights, I thought it would be best to participate as much as possible.

Time flew by as I lived my busy yet rewarding days to the fullest, and before I knew it, December 25 had arrived. It was Christmas Day. Lia and I returned to the dorm after class, put down our things, and got ready. By the time we were done, it was five in the afternoon, one hour until the Christmas party.

"Hmm-hmm-hmm!"

I could hear Lia humming happily in her room. She was more excited about the celebration than anyone I knew. And she hadn't had a bite to eat since morning; if I knew her, she was going to try every single dish at the buffet.

Every student in school is going to be there… I'm a little scared about whatever Shii is plotting, but I'm looking forward to sharing this party with all of my classmates.

I put the present I'd bought in Aurest in a bag and got ready to go out.

"Ta-da! How do I look?" Lia asked after emerging from her room in a Santa hat. She stared intently at me to gauge my reaction. The hat, with its red fabric and the fluffy white ball on the tip, was adorable on her.

"You look really nice in it," I replied.

"R-really? Hee-hee, thanks." She smiled and blushed. "Show me yours, Allen!"

"O-okay..." Urged on by Lia, I put on the headpiece I'd been given. "Wh-what do you think?"

It was a reindeer headband with two antlers.

"It's so cute! You pull it off very well," Lia said.

"R-really...?"

I stared at myself in the full-length mirror. *I don't know about this...* I was wearing the reindeer antlers along with my cool Thousand Blade uniform. As far I was concerned, it was terribly mismatched. *Why can't the guys wear Santa hats, too? It's not fair...*

Thousand Blade Academy had distributed the Santa hats to all the girls and the reindeer headbands to all the guys. The dress code for the party left no room for doubt about this stipulation. *This is so embarrassing... But I'm wearing these antlers to go to the party with Lia. I can put up with it if I think about it like that.*

"Let's go," I said after we checked to make sure we hadn't forgotten anything.

"Okay!" Lia responded.

We left the dorm and headed for Thousand Blade's auditorium.

■

The entrance to the auditorium was crowded with antlered boys and girls in Santa hats.

"Let's see... Reception's over here, Lia," I said.

"O-okay!" she responded.

I grabbed her by the hand so she wouldn't get sucked into the crowd and walked to the simple tent set up for registration. We joined one of the four lines and reached the desk five minutes later.

"Please show me your student ID and gift," the female receptionist requested. I placed both of the items she'd requested on the desk. "Thank you very much, Allen Rodol and Lia Vesteria... Here, let me give you these name tags."

She attached a small name tag with a stylish butterfly pattern to one of my antlers and did the same for Lia's hat.

"Those name tags have a number you'll need to use to identify yourselves in the auditorium and to reenter. Be careful not to lose them. I'll also be taking your presents for the grand gift exchange that will be held during the party. Merry Christmas!" the receptionist cheered, ringing a bell.

"Merry Christmas," I responded.

"Merry Christmas!" Lia echoed.

After finishing at reception, we followed the crowd into the auditorium where the dazzling party venue sprawled out before us. My eyes snapped to the magnificent Christmas tree, which was decorated with tinsel that resembled snow, colorful lights, and a splendid star. It was by far the most opulent holiday tree I had ever seen. The auditorium was also decorated with golden Christmas bells, shining ribbons, and heart-shaped balloons. A dignified chandelier hanging from the ceiling provided the festivities with a warm ambiance.

"This is insane," I remarked.

"Wow, it's so pretty!" Lia exclaimed.

She and I marveled at the venue's extravagant atmosphere.

"Welcome, Allen and Lia!"

Shii came up to us from the back of the auditorium wearing a delightful Santa costume.

"Wow, you look so cute!" Lia gushed.

"It looks really nice on you," I said, giving my honest opinion. It wasn't flattery to say that Shii totally pulled off her red and white outfit.

"Thanks. You look adorable in your Santa hat, Lia. And...hee-hee, those antlers are a perfect fit for you, Allen," Shii responded, looking up at my headband and giggling.

"Ah-ha-ha, I'm not sure how to feel about that..." I doubted many people would be thrilled to be told they looked good wearing reindeer antlers.

"I'm just messing with you. I still have some preparations to make, so I'll talk to you later," Shii said before slipping away toward the back of the auditorium.

...She's acting weirdly normal. Based on her behavior just then, it didn't seem like she was plotting anything. *But I can't let my guard down. Shii is mischievous to her core. I have to remain alert, or I could end up in a world of pain.*

A tap on my shoulder brought me out of my thoughts. It was Rose, wearing a Santa hat.

"Merry Christmas, Rose," I said in greeting.

"Merry Christmas!" she responded, just before someone collided into my back.

"Whoops," the person said. "Hmph, it's you, maggot. You make the wimpiest deer I've ever seen."

It was Claude, also wearing a Santa hat. She'd clearly bumped into me on purpose. I knew the antlers did me no favors, so there was no point in arguing otherwise.

"You look cute in that Santa hat, Claude," I responded.

"Hm?! I-I don't want to hear you call me 'cute' ever again, maggot! I'll slice those deer antlers off your head!" she yelled, blushing and glaring at me.

"Hey! Give it a rest, Claude! Those are *reindeer* antlers, not deer antlers!" Lia corrected, sounding fed up.

I appreciate Lia standing up for me, but that's not what offended me. I would rather she tell Claude to stop calling me "maggot."

"My deepest apologies, Your Highness…," Claude said. I was losing track of how many exchanges we'd had like this one.

Moments later, the lights dimmed, and a stage at the end of the auditorium was brightly illuminated.

"Hello, everyone! Are you ready for a Christmas to remember? Let's forget all our troubles and kick back tonight! Merry Christmas!" Shii announced, signaling the start of the party.

""""Merry Christmas!"""" the students responded.

As soon as Shii finished speaking, school employees brought out an enormous amount of food and set it on tables along the front of the auditorium. I saw meat and seafood dishes, assorted vegetables, clear soup, juicy fruit, and other fancy foods I didn't even know the names of.

It smells heavenly, I thought as enticing aromas drifted toward me from every which way. *There are a lot of students here… Isn't it gonna be chaos if they put out this much food at once?* Contrary to my expectations, however, I looked around and saw that my fellow students were perfectly calm. The atmosphere in the auditorium remained warm and lively as people chatted with their friends, ordered drinks, and filled their plates in moderation.

That makes sense, actually. Almost everyone here was nobility or a member of a respected family. Unlike me, they were probably used to extravagant buffets. That would explain their restraint.

"I-it's time, Allen! Let's grab some grub before it's all gone!" Lia urged, unable to contain her excitement. Seeing this princess—the highest-ranking person in the venue—act as she normally did put me at ease.

"Yeah, let's do it," I said with a soft laugh. I followed her as she raced toward the table and grabbed a plate.

This tableware looks really expensive… The dish I picked up was as shiny as a mirror and had a golden scrollwork pattern along the edge.

I didn't have a good eye for value, but it had to be absurdly pricey. *I need to be careful not to drop it.*

Feeling a little nervous, I filled my plate with a good balance of main and side dishes. Meanwhile, Lia stacked hers with an array of filling foods, including meat-filled ramzac. Rose picked out whatever she fancied, which turned out to be mostly fruit and sweet desserts. Claude got nothing but meat, grabbing her portions with practiced hands. You could learn a lot about a person just by looking at their plate.

Once we finished getting our food, we gathered at a spot that wasn't crowded and dug in.

"These vegetables are so fresh!" I said.

"Mmm! Ramzac remains undefeated!" Lia exclaimed.

"This ice cream is perfectly sweet!" Rose remarked.

"Mm, this meat isn't half bad," Claude muttered.

Elegant, orchestral music began to play as we ate. I looked toward the stage and saw a large group of musicians playing a wide variety of instruments.

"Hmm... This is the Leevethive Symphony's Fourth Movement," Lia said, naming the song seconds after the orchestra started playing.

"Wow, do you know a lot about music?" I asked.

"Hah, of course she does! Princess Lia is a highly educated lady befitting her station, and she's knowledgeable in all subjects!" Claude answered for her, proudly puffing out her chest. She looked delighted to have gotten the opportunity to praise her lady.

We spent the next while chatting as we listened to the orchestra—which was famous even in Aurest—and marveling at a giant Christmas cake that was set out, along with watching Lia panic and rush to get more food whenever she ran out. It was a very fun time. After about an hour, Shii took the stage.

"It's time to start the eagerly anticipated grand gift exchange!" she declared. The black curtain behind her rose to reveal a mountain of presents. These must have been the presents my peers and I had bought.

"There's so many...," I said.

There were one hundred and eighty students in each year, which meant there were five hundred and forty presents in total. *How are they planning on distributing all these gifts?* Handing them out one by one would take forever.

"Class 1-A, please come to the stage," Shii instructed with her clear, carrying voice.

"That's us," I said.

"Hee-hee, I wonder what kind of present I'm gonna get!" Lia responded.

"Yeah, me too," I said.

We walked to the stage. There were ten boxes set in front of it with "lottery" written on them.

"Each lottery box contains strips of paper with numbers on them. The number signifies what present you will receive," Shii announced.

I looked closely at the presents and saw that each had a small tag attached.

"Oh, it's totally random," Lia said.

"Yeah, looks like it," I replied.

My classmates and I all drew from the lottery boxes. I got number forty-one.

"Have you all drawn, Class 1-A? Please lift your number overhead!" Shii instructed.

I did as she said, and thirty presents flew through the air toward us.

""""Whoa!""""

Someone must have done that with remote-controlled Soul Attire. I looked around and found a female student wielding a rapier at the wing of the stage. It seemed like she was the one sending the presents through the air.

"Guess this one's mine," I said after catching a present marked with a forty-one. *Huh? This package looks familiar... Well, I might as well open it.*

I carefully unwrapped it and opened the box to reveal a small yellow stuffed animal.

This is one of the ugliest dolls I've ever seen... I can't even tell what it is. I think it's a tiger...or maybe a fox? It must be one of those ugly-cute things..., I thought, studying my handmade toy with mixed feelings.

"Hey, is this your present?" Lia asked, holding a wooden sword.

"Yeah, definitely. That's the wooden sword I bought," I confirmed.

I could say that with confidence because of the packaging at her feet, which I identified right away since I'd made it myself. The store where I'd bought it from refused to provide packaging, so I had to take matters into my own hands.

"Ah-ha-ha, I knew it! You're the only one who would think to buy a wooden sword as a present," Lia said.

"Y-you think so...?" I responded. Was I supposed to take that as praise?

"Thank you, I'll treasure it!" Lia said, looking at the sword happily. I was glad to see she liked it.

"That would make me happy. Um... Is this your present?" I asked, showing Lia the weird stuffed animal I'd received. Given the...unique nature of the plushie, and the fact that it was in the same packaging that Lia had brought with her on the way to the auditorium, I was fairly certain it was hers.

"Hey, that's my bear!" she exclaimed.

"It's a bear...?"

"I found it while out shopping for gifts. Isn't it adorable?"

"S-sure..."

So this yellow monstrosity is a bear... I stared at it.

"How'd you realize it was mine?" Lia asked, cocking her head curiously.

"Because I couldn't think of anyone else who would pick such an ug—*ahem*, unique doll."

"Ha-ha, isn't it great?"

"Yeah, thank you. I love it."

This stuffed animal would clearly damage the aesthetic of any room you placed it in, but I didn't care. It was from Lia, so I was going to display it as prominently as I could.

"What crazy odds," I said.

There were five hundred and forty students in the school, but we happened to get each other's presents... The chances of that were incredibly miniscule.

"Ha-ha, right?" Lia responded, laughing shyly.

Having collected our presents, we shared what we got with Rose, Claude, and all of our classmates, which put us into an even more festive mood.

■

The clock struck eight in the evening. Shii, who had been darting about the venue all night, once again took the stage.

"*Ahem*—Listen up, everyone! Now that the grand gift exchange has left us feeling all warm and cozy, it's time for the main event—the annual Crush Your Crush Competition!" she declared.

"Let's gooooo! I've been waiting so long for this!"

"A-Allen's gonna be really popular, isn't he...?"

"Get that timid attitude out of here! Girls need to be brave! What's the worst that could happen?"

"Urgh, I don't want the embarrassment of being rejected..."

"Heh, I'm going after Princess Lia! My love for her will be unstoppable!"

"Dude, you're asking for a swift death. Lia's gonna be the most difficult girl to get on campus. Watch out for Allen if you value your life..."

The second and third years grew very excited.

"Crush...your crush?"

"What's that?"

The first years, on the other hand, had no idea what was going on.

Shii said this is an annual event. That must mean it was also held last year, which would explain why the upperclassmen are excited while the first years are out of the loop. What kind of competition is this? I wondered.

I met eyes with Shii, and she gave me a wide smile and a small wave. *Oh... This is what she was talking about.* The Crush Your Crush Competition must have been the "little event" she'd mentioned earlier this month.

Now that I think about it, Shii's been busy the entire party. I haven't seen Lilim or Tirith, either. They've probably been up to no good the whole time while everyone else was enjoying the festivities. I'm gonna have to do this, aren't I...?

I couldn't skip a school event, and Shii, Lilim, and Tirith worked hard to set this up. I would definitely feel bad if I refused to participate.

It's eight PM, so this is probably the final event of the Christmas party. It was time to put a nice bow on this festive Christmas night.

Okay... Let's do this.

I stretched to relieve the tension and readied myself for the Crush Your Crush Competition.

■

Shii smiled boldly and explained the rules of the Crush Your Crush Competition.

"The rules are simple. The objective for the boys is to take a girl's Santa hat, and the objective for the girls is to take a boy's reindeer antlers! Once a couple exchanges their hats, they are required to become boyfriend and girlfriend!"

"Excuse me?!" I exclaimed. I couldn't believe what I'd just heard.

"You have a time limit of one hour, and you cannot leave the Thousand

Blade campus. Other than that, anything goes! You may use your Soul Attire, team up with other people, share information, or use any other advantage you like! This event is a school tradition, so participation is mandatory!" Shii continued.

Thousand Blade's absurd traditions never ceased to amaze me. *I need to make sure no one takes Lia's hat!*

"Before we kick things off, I have one last important announcement! I'm offering the entirety of the Student Council's budget to the club of whoever takes the headband of Allen Rodol from Class 1-A!" Shii proclaimed.

"P-President?!" I shouted.

A great many eyes turned toward me, most of them belonging to the members of the Swordcraft Club. I had heard they were struggling with the paltry budget they'd been saddled with from losing early in the Club Budget War. Lust colored their expressions at the prospect of obtaining the highest allotment of funds in the school.

"Please wait, President! That would put me at too much of a disad—," I began, but Shii cut me off.

"The Crush Your Crush Competition starts now!" she declared joyfully.

The Swordcraft Club immediately surrounded me, led by their president, Jean Bael, and their vice president, Sirtie Rosette.

"I hate dancing to that witch's strings, but we're never gonna get another chance like this! We're taking Allen Rodol down, for the survival of the Swordcraft Club!" Jean shouted.

"Ha-ha-ha! I'm gonna get you back for our match during the Recruiting Period!" Sirtie proclaimed.

There's so many of them... Over one hundred students had surrounded me, and more were coming. I quickly drew my sword, assumed the middle stance, and looked at Lia.

"P-Princess Lia! Your Santa hat is mine!" a boy shouted.

"No! I won't let you have it!" Lia screamed. She had been surrounded by a crowd of male students.

"Rose, would you honor me with a match?" a boy asked.

"Ha, that sounds fun... Take my hat if you can!" Rose answered. A large number of male students had gathered around her too.

"C-Claude! Will you please go out with me?!" a girl shouted.

"Hold on! I'm a girl!" Claude shouted back. She had been surrounded by a pack of female students.

Around thirty people had encircled Lia, Rose, and Claude each. There were over one hundred students around me. Multiple sword fights had already broken out in the auditorium.

So much for the peaceful Christmas party... Thousand Blade never stayed quiet for long.

I need to get out of the auditorium. I'm at too much of a disadvantage in here. The crowd obstructed my vision, and there were countless places where someone could hide to perform a surprise attack. Considering that all anyone needed to do to defeat me was take my antlers, it was imperative that I avoid the mob and get outside where I would have an unobstructed view of my surroundings.

"Lia, Rose, Claude, I'm going outside!" I shouted.

"Okay!" Lia responded.

"Understood," Rose said.

"Hmph, it seems you realize the disadvantages of fighting in a confined space," Claude grumbled.

Our battles began after they all responded. I ran to the entrance of the auditorium while fending off the approaching Swordcraft Club members and stopped just before I went outside.

"Lia! Don't let anyone take your hat, okay?" I yelled. It was embarrassing, but I had to say it.

"...! Okay! I won't!" she said reassuringly.

I dashed out of the auditorium after hearing her reply.

"Damn it... After him!" Jean commanded.

"""Okay!""" the Swordcraft Club members responded.

■

I ran from the auditorium to the schoolyard and assumed the middle stance.

Okay... My vision is completely unobstructed out here. I couldn't ask for a better place to fight such a huge crowd. Man, this is a wild sight..., I thought as over one hundred Swordcraft Club members surrounded me. Each and every one of them was wielding their Soul Attire and watching me carefully.

Jean addressed his club members. "Listen up! We're facing Allen Rodol. Don't even *think* of trying to defeat him! We're not up to it, no matter how many of us take him on! Remember, the only thing we have to do is get his antlers!"

"""Okay!""" his club members responded.

Their strategy was to abandon trying to best me in a fair fight and instead focus on taking my antlers. That was going to make this difficult.

"Sirtie and I will do our best to repress Allen's darkness! Use the window we give you to snag those antlers!" Jean yelled.

"""Okay!"""

Jean sneered and pointed his sword at me. "Don't even think of accusing us of foul play."

"I wouldn't dream of it," I responded.

This event was designed to produce chaotic melees. I couldn't blame him for acting within the rules.

"Allen can produce four of those mighty dark tentacles at a time. Sirtie, can you take two of them?" Jean asked.

"You bet!" Sirtie responded.

Having sorted out their strategy, Jean and Sirtie dashed toward me.

"Let's do this, Allen! Fang Chain Style—Decastrike!" Jean yelled, unleashing ten quick slashes.

"You're not beating me this time! Open Circle Style—Circle of Fire!" Sirtie screamed, performing a blazing hot thrust.

I summoned my cloak of gloom to defend myself.

"This must be the defensive darkness I've heard about. It's even tougher than I expected...," Jean said.

"It covered his whole body immediately! That's not fair!" Sirtie whined.

My barrier blocked their attacks completely, allowing me to counter.

"Dark Shadow!" I shouted. Ten tentacles branched off from my massive well of shadows and raced toward my two opponents, each one pulsing as if alive.

"Th-there they are!" Jean said.

"Hey, there weren't supposed to be that many!" Sirtie shouted.

They and the rest of the Swordcraft Club members flinched at the sight of the bizarre darkness.

"The amount of tentacles I can control at once increased from four to ten recently. Don't accuse *me* of foul play, okay?" I said.

"Grk... Allen's just a first-year! Summon your pride as upperclassmen and charge!" Jean yelled.

""""YEEEAAAHHH!"""" the hundred-plus Swordcraft Club members responded, joining together and surging toward me.

But a few minutes later...

"I can't believe we didn't even scratch him..."

"Ha, ha-ha... No one should be...that strong..."

...the gasping Swordcraft Club members lay sprawled out on the schoolyard beneath the moonlight.

"Sure enough, Dark Shadow is my best move for fighting a crowd of opponents," I said to myself. I defeated them all using the ten tentacles without even having to swing my blade once.

I had broken through the first wave of opponents, but it didn't take long for the second wave—consisting of three girls—to appear.

"I-I'm Lina Hashwalt from Class 3-D! I've always had a thing for you, Allen! Would you please go out with me?"

"I'm Farrah Salitaire from Class 2-B! I love your gentle strength and that cool darkness... C-can I be your girlfriend?"

"Shady Soote, Class 2-A. I fell for you when I witnessed your untiring dedication to practice swings. I request that we embark on a serious relationship."

All three girls blushed as they spoke. I couldn't believe my ears, but their expressions were as serious as could be. None of them were joking.

"Um... I'm sorry," I responded, bowing my head in apology. I appreciated their confessions, but that was the only answer I could give.

"Wh-why?!"

"Will you at least give me a reason?!"

"I would like an explanation."

The three girls refused to back down.

They opened up and shared their real feelings with me. It would be rude to not respond in kind.

"Because...there's already someone I like," I admitted, feeling myself blush.

"N-no..."

"I-it's okay, girls... There's no need to panic yet!"

"We just have to take him by force!"

The three stared at me with determination.

"Surrender and give me those antlers!"

"I'll never give up..."

"Prepare yourself!"

The girls quickly drew their swords and ran at me with harrowing resolve.

"I guess this was unavoidable...," I muttered.

I reluctantly drew my sword, deflected their slashes, and hit them each on the back of the neck hard enough to knock them out.

"Phew... I'm done here," I said with relief, just before detecting a frigid, malicious presence behind me. "Huh?!" I instantly ducked to the left, narrowly avoiding a merciless thrust.

"Shoot, I almost had you."

"There you are, President."

I turned around to find Shii Arkstoria, looking frustrated that her attempt to cut off my antlers failed.

"Greetings, Allen. How are you doing?" she asked.

"Wonderful, no thanks to you," I jabbed lightly.

"Tee-hee, glad to hear it," she said with a giggle.

Is she not cold? I thought with concern. She had to have been freezing in this December weather with the amount of skin her Santa outfit left bare.

"Mwa-ha-ha! You'd better not forget about us, Allen!"

"We're getting you back for the Shadow Thousand Blade Festival!"

Lilim and Tirith, who I hadn't seen once in the auditorium, stepped up beside Shii.

"We're doing this three-on-one, huh? You're really not holding back this time," I said.

The duo had given me a hard fight when I faced them together during the Shadow Thousand Blade Festival. Adding Shii to the mix would make this a very difficult challenge.

"Hee-hee, would you expect anything less? I've never beaten you at a single thing. First it was the Club Budget War, then poker, then cheating at poker—as the heir to the renowned Arkstoria family, I won't tolerate any more losing!" Shii declared, her expression turning uncharacteristically serious. Then she extended her hand into the air. "Trace—Aqua Queen!"

Shii pulled a beautiful sword out of a rift in the air. It was blue as the sky and clear as the ocean. She gripped the handle gently and assumed a perfect guard.

"Your legendary undefeated record ends here," she said.

"Taste the might of your Student Council seniors!" Lilim shouted.

"We can't lose, no matter what it takes…!" Tirith added.

The three of them stared at me with a competitive fire in their eyes.

"Okay… You may outnumber me, but I have no intention of getting bested," I responded. I summoned my mock black sword, which was coated with darkness, and assumed the middle stance.

I studied Shii's Soul Attire, Aqua Queen. *I saw it multiple times during the Sword Master Festival, but I still find it breathtakingly beautiful…* The blade was perfectly clear, and it sported a bold and intricate pattern that conveyed great strength. It was so gorgeous, I could stare at it for hours.

"Okay, time to recover our dignity as upperclassmen! Pummel—Bursting Clay!" Lilim shouted.

"Defeat isn't an option… Bind—Psychic Shackle!"

Lilim and Tirith summoned their Soul Attires simultaneously.

They're not messing around…

I'd gotten a full taste of Lilim and Tirith's Soul Attires during the Shadow Thousand Blade Festival. Bursting Clay had the ability to produce explosive earth. It was simple, but incredibly powerful. I would need to be especially careful not to lose track of Lilim.

Psychic Shackle had the formidable power to bind and control anything in sight. It was only moderately strong, but its versatility was a pain to deal with. It would be best to defeat Tirith quickly.

Dealing with just Bursting Clay and Psychic Shackle at the same time would be hard enough, but I'll have to manage against Shii's Aqua Queen as well… These girls were three of the best swordfighters at Thousand Blade. Fighting all of them at once was going to be difficult.

That Christmas party was so much fun. I just wanted to take it easy tonight…, I thought, sighing internally. It would be easy to use Dark Shadow to flee, but I knew I would regret doing that later. Shii had really been looking forward to this event, and she'd spent most of the

Christmas party preparing for it. All her hard work would be for nothing if I ran. She would pout like never before.

In order to actually win and save myself future pain, I need to accept their match in spite of the dire numbers disadvantage, walk right into their trap, and overcome it. This is going to be quite the challenge.

"Hmm-hmm, even *you* have to see how hopeless this is, Allen. Do you want to surrender?" Shii asked boastfully.

"No... I think I'd regret doing that," I answered.

"Huh? What do you mean?" she asked, looking confused.

"Never mind. Let's not waste any more time," I said.

"That's what I want to hear," Shii responded.

"Mwa-ha-ha, it's time to teach you a lesson you'll never forget!" Lilim shouted.

"You're going down this time!" Tirith declared.

I locked eyes with Shii. Our respective gazes were so intense that sparks seemed to fly between us.

They have a three-to-one advantage. A defensive strategy will only harm me in the long run. I need to be aggressive and strike first! I thought.

I covered my legs with jet-black darkness and entered striking range of Tirith in a single step.

"Huh?!"

Her face went pale—I was close enough to deliver a finishing blow, and I had already raised my mock black sword overhead.

Lilim is skilled at close combat, and Shii is skilled at both ranged and close combat. I can leave them for later. Tirith only specializes in ranged combat, so removing her will make it much easier to gain control of the fight!

I brought down my blade as hard as I could.

"That's not...good enough...!" Tirith gasped, jumping to the left to dodge my slash.

"You're not going anywhere," I said, responding quickly enough to stop my swing, step to the side, and pursue her with an angled flourish.

"What the… How did you react so quickly?!" Tirith cried, shutting her eyes.

"Not so fast!"

"Not happening, bud!"

Shii and Lilim slashed at me from behind in sync.

"Damn…," I muttered. Abandoning my attack, I whipped my sword around horizontally to defend myself, locking blades with Shii and Lilim.

"Haaaaaaaa!" Shii yelled.

"Graaaaaah!" Lilim screamed.

They both put all their weight behind their weapons, but my arm strength far surpassed theirs.

"*Hraagh!*" I growled.

"Gaaah!" Shii screamed.

"No freaking way!" Lilim shouted.

I knocked them off their feet, but they managed to land in a graceful roll. Tirith joined back up with them a moment later, having used the opportunity to collect herself. Our first exchange had ended in a draw.

"Tirith, are you okay?" Shii asked.

"That was almost light's out for you," Lilim said.

"I thought I was finished, to be honest… Thanks for saving me…," Tirith muttered.

They kept their eyes trained on me as they spoke.

"I can't believe he bested me and Lilim together…," Shii said.

"He doesn't even feel human anymore…," Lilim commented.

"There's no way we can beat him in a contest of strength…," Tirith grumbled.

I decided to work out my strategy while they discussed theirs. *Taking one of them out has to be my first priority.* As our initial exchange had just demonstrated, I was at a significant disadvantage fighting on my own against three opponents. This duel could get out of hand if I didn't eliminate one of them quickly.

Time to step things up.

"Dark Shadow!" I yelled, cloaking my body in pitch-black darkness and spreading ten tendrils far and wide.

"Well, we knew this was coming...," Shii groaned.

"We just saw him use it against the Swordcraft Club, but it's so much more overwhelming up close...," Lilim responded.

"He looks way too gentle to wield such a wicked power...," Tirith muttered.

The three Student Council members gulped as they watched the darkness undulate before them.

"We have the numbers advantage, but don't forget who we're up against. We can't take Allen's strength lightly. Let's give him everything we've got, Lilim and Tirith!" Shii instructed.

"You bet! It would be sooo embarrassing if he beat us one-on-three!" Lilim insisted.

"Our honor's on the line...!" Tirith said.

Looking reenergized, the three of them brandished their Soul Attires.

"Aqua Garden!" Shii shouted, lifting her sword high and summoning a giant ball of water above her head. Her Soul Attire had complete command of water, which she could use to create an infinite variety of attacks.

"Burst Sword!" Lilim yelled, as gray-brown clay covered her Soul Attire. The dangerous earth would explode against anything her weapon connected with.

"Psychic Threads!" Tirith shouted, swinging her Soul Attire to spread tiny threads of spirit power everywhere. The threads attached themselves to the Swordcraft Club members' blades, which were scattered throughout the schoolyard, and lifted over one hundred of them into the air. I wasn't looking forward to dodging them all at once.

"The real fight begins now, Allen!" Shii declared.

"Underestimate us at your peril," Lilim warned.

"It's finally time to get revenge...!" Tirith said.

Now that they were ready to get serious, they each moved to the range they were most skilled from. Lilim took a step forward to engage me in close combat, Shii stayed where she was because she could handle combat at any distance, and Tirith jumped far back to fight from range.

"Heh, hope you're ready!" Lilim said, quickly closing the gap between us. "Take this!" She swung her clay-packed sword at me with tremendous force.

Burst Sword creates a directional explosion upon impact, so I won't be able to defend against it like normal. It's supremely effective in close combat, but I'm ready for it.

I slashed my blade diagonally to meet her downward swing.

"Heh. Explode!" Lilim shouted when our swords collided. Her weapon detonated, sending a massive blast and searing heat my way.

"Dark Box!" I yelled, summoning a sphere of darkness to trap Lilim's blade and suppress the violent eruption.

"What was that…?!" she gasped, widening her eyes in astonishment at how easily I'd blocked Burst Sword.

"Don't look away from your opponent," I said, swinging my blade up at hers with moderate strength.

"Huh?!" she yelled as I knocked Bursting Clay out of her hands and into the air. "Crap…"

Now unarmed, Lilim turned and ran to recover her blade. But I wasn't going to let her do that.

"Dark Shadow!" I cried, summoning three tentacles with the goal of knocking her unconscious.

"Tirith!" Shii called out.

"I'm already on it! Psychic Threads!" Tirith yelled, extending forth threads of spirit power.

"Huh…," I muttered as the threads wrapped around Dark Shadow, slightly hindering its movement.

"How are these things so heavy? Hurry up, Lilim…," Tirith said, struggling.

"I know, I know!" Lilim responded. She sprinted for her sword, which had plunged into the schoolyard lawn.

I won't let her reach it! I thought. *I can control ten tendrils at a time. They've hindered three of them, but I've still got seven left!* I turned toward Lilim as she reached desperately for her sword and sent my remaining seven tentacles rushing toward her.

"Not on my watch! Aqua Trick!" Shii shouted. The water above her head morphed into a variety of weapons—including swords, axes, spears, shields, sickles—that all shot toward me simultaneously. It was no ordinary water that Shii's Soul Attire had summoned, but steel water, which was kneaded with dense spirit power to make it harder than iron.

"Shoot..." I grunted and reluctantly retracted the tendrils of shadow I'd sent after Lilim to defend myself against the deluge of weapons. Lilim used the opportunity to recover her Soul Attire and quickly rejoin Shii and Tirith.

"My bad, I lost focus...," she said, her expression turning bitter. Sweat beaded on her forehead. "But man, I'm stunned Allen was able to suppress that giant explosion... That darkness of his is beyond insane."

"There's no way he can maintain that level of output for long, though... Maybe we should try to exhaust his spirit power?" Tirith suggested.

"Fat chance of that happening. I've heard that Allen has more spirit power than Black Fist. Can you picture him exhausted? I sure can't," Shii said.

""Neither can I...,"" Lilim and Tirith responded.

They all observed me as they whispered to each other.

"Let's all attack him at once. You both remember the spot, right?" Shii asked.

"Oh, right! Of course!" Lilim said.

"Need you even ask?" Tirith responded.

"Let's do this!" Shii exclaimed.

"Heck yeah!" Lilim shouted.

"Understood!" Tirith said.

There was a renewed determination in their eyes. *They're probably about to spring their trap. I don't know what they were doing during the Christmas party, but these three are some of the most competitive people I know. Whatever they set up is going to be trouble.*

I braced myself.

"Here we go! Burst Rain!" Lilim shouted. She swung her sword horizontally, spreading mushy clay into the air.

"Psychic Threads!" Tirith yelled. The hundred-plus blades she was controlling flew toward the explosive earth, which coated their blades to turn them all into Burst Swords.

They're combining their Soul Attire abilities... They were already hard enough to deal with individually. It would be nigh-impossible to stave off over a hundred airborne Burst Swords. I watched Tirith with utmost caution.

"Aqua Blade!" Shii shouted, absorbing the giant body of water above her head into her blade.

I studied her weapon closely. *It looks like she's enveloped her blade in high-pressure water, like Raine's Aqua Robe technique. It's safe to assume that sharpened her sword.*

"Take this—Aqua Slash!"

Shii swung quickly, sending a sharp arc of water toward me.

"So you can perform projectile slash attacks. Haaa!" I shouted, trying to deflect the attack.

"Hee-hee. Expand!" Shii yelled. The Aqua Slash suddenly burst open before me, turning into a heavy fog that enveloped the area.

Oh, she was trying to obscure my vision... I don't know what they're planning, but things will definitely go sideways if I stay put.

I tried to escape from the fog, but my path was cut off by Burst Swords that started to rain down on me.

"Are you kidding me...?" I muttered in disbelief. The blades struck the ground in a series of massive explosions. I immediately wrapped a cloak of darkness around myself to mitigate the impacts, but there were too many explosions to prevent injury entirely. Red filled my vision as the Burst Swords carpet bombed me, wounding me as fiery wind and shock waves smothered me from every which way. I needed to escape this.

"Haaaaaaaaa!" I screamed, sending darkness out all around me to knock down the Burst Swords floating in the air.

"P-pull back!" Lilim shouted.

"We're done if he so much as grazes us...," Tirith muttered.

They both retreated to safety to avoid my wide-reaching, indiscriminate attack.

"Got you!" Shii yelled immediately afterward, tearing through the fog as she jumped at me from behind.

That was well-executed..., I thought. I had sent most of my shadows into the sky, leaving myself only lightly guarded. Shii couldn't have picked a better time to strike. *Unfortunately for her, she's not fast enough.*

I ducked just before her sharp thrust reached my back.

"What?!" Shii shouted in disbelief.

I had fought Shido, who was gifted with special physical prowess, and Idora, who gained explosive speed from her Flying Thunder ability. Compared to those two, Shii's speed was lacking.

"You're done," I said, slashing at her chest with my sword. But something felt wrong. "Is this...a clone made of water?!"

"Ding-ding-ding! That's correct!" Shii said. Her voice came from behind me. "Your prize is a taste of my steel!"

"Ngh..."

I spun around and dodged her slash by a paper-thin margin...

"Nice reaction time."

...but she thrust a foot into my left side with a roundhouse kick, sending me flying through the air.

"Grk...!"

I quickly scanned for the girls' locations before I landed. They weren't pursuing me. *I had no idea that she could make clones. What* can't *water-control Soul Attire do...?*

Shii barked an order as I fell gracefully to the ground. "We've got him! Now, Lilim!"

"Okay!" Lilim shouted. She plunged her sword into the schoolyard, and the ground exploded around me in a circle.

"Huh?!" I gasped as I fell into the hole. *Th-this was the trap?!* A shocking amount of explosive clay was packed into the bottom of it. This must have been what they were working on during the Christmas party.

"Hmm-hmm, this is over! Aqua Trick!" Shii yelled. Weapons made of water raced toward me, covering the width of the hole.

This is really bad... Armaments were raining down on me from above, and explosive clay awaited me below. I was about to be in a world of hurt if I didn't do something.

"Dark Shadow!" I shouted, summoning ten dark tentacles and sending them above and below. I cleared away the water weapons and tried to engulf the explosive clay, but...

"Did you really think I was going to let you do that? Psychic Chains, full strength!"

...Tirith produced tough chains to obstruct my darkness.

What the heck?!

The chains were much thicker and stronger than the threads she'd produced before; she must have used every last drop of her spirit power to create them. The binds completely hindered Dark Shadow for a period of milliseconds, which normally wouldn't have mattered, but I was in a critically dangerous situation. Those fractions of a second could mean the difference between life and death.

Crap, I'm not gonna escape...

"You're finished!" Shii declared.

"We win this time!" Lilim cheered.

"Our strategy worked perfectly!" Tirith said.

Their victorious cries carried down into the dark hole. *Those three truly are formidable swordswomen. They make a perfect team, too, each covering for one another's weaknesses. They did an excellent job combining their abilities to form an effective strategy. The old me probably would've lost to them.*

That's right—the old *me. Guess I have no choice...*

I sheathed my blade and reached my hand into the air.

"Destroy—Rapacious Demon Zeon!" I yelled, summoning a violent gale of darkness.

"Ahhh!" Shii screamed.

"Wh-what's that?!" Lilim shouted.

"Allen cut through my Psychic Chains!" Tirith yelled.

An abyss of blackness swallowed their three-part attack, including the liquid armaments, the explosive clay, and the thick chains.

"You gave me a real scare."

"""...?!"""

I broke out of their trap and escaped from the hole uninjured. In my hand was the true black sword—the manifestation of my Spirit Core's power.

"No way..." Shii gasped.

"H-hey, I haven't heard about this...," Lilim said.

"This is bad news...," Tirith muttered.

The three of them went pale and faltered back a step.

"Since when did you manifest your Soul Attire, Allen?!" Shii asked.

"I got roped into an incident a while back... Things got a little dangerous, and I ended up attaining my Soul Attire," I answered evasively. I couldn't be candid about my trip to Daglio because Clown had sworn me to secrecy.

"Lilim, Tirith... I doubt I need to tell you this, but that ebon blade is really dangerous...," Shii said.

"Yeah, just looking at it is giving me chills... But we can't quit now," Lilim responded.

"I want to run, personally... I already spent most of my spirit power on Psychic Chains...," Tirith muttered.

They all shifted their weight backward and assumed defensive stances.

I gulped, floored anew at the overwhelming waves of power Zeon projected. It had been over a month since I'd summoned it. *This sword is absurd...* The entirety of the weapon was pitch-black, including its blade, hilt, and guard. It was less a blade and more a mass of might that had been forced into the shape of one.

I feel light, like I've suddenly grown wings, and darkness is surging from deep within my body! There were so many shadows that I felt like I needed to expel them or risk my body bursting.

"Okay... Time to go on the offensive," I said before taking one step forward.

""""..."""""

The girls wordlessly stepped back in response.

I need to go after Tirith first. I don't want her restricting my movement with her threads and chains of spirit power again.

I turned toward her and lightly kicked off the ground. My vision blurred, and before I knew it, I was behind her.

""H-he disappeared?!"" Lilim and Tirith shouted, shocked.

"Behind you, Tirith!" Shii warned. She was the only one who reacted in time, but she was still too late.

"That's one down," I said, striking Tirith hard in the back of the head with my hilt.

"Wha?!" she cried out before collapsing silently to the ground.

I kicked off the ground again, ending up at Lilim's side.

"Dodge, Lilim!" Shii yelled in vain.

"That's two down," I said, kicking Lilim hard in the side.

"Gah?!" She gasped as I sent her flying horizontally through the air like a ball until she crashed into the wall of the main school building.

...Was that overkill? I'd only wanted to kick her hard enough to knock her unconscious, not send her soaring across campus. *I need to work*

on reining in my strength, I thought, making a mental note to sneak over and heal Lilim's injuries later.

Having knocked out Tirith and Lilim in seconds flat, I turned toward Shii. "It's one-on-one now."

"I had no idea you were hiding this level of power... You really are a naughty boy," Shii said.

"Hey, I wasn't hiding anything. I just didn't have a chance to use it."

"Hmph, a likely story."

Shii glared daggers at me.

I need to get this over with. A good while had passed since this crazy event started, and I'd been beside myself with worry for Lia the entire time. *I would never say this to her face, but she can be pretty airheaded.* Her skill with the blade was unparalleled, but it was rather easy to catch her off guard. I wanted to go to her aid as soon as possible, just in case.

I held the black sword at my navel and assumed the middle stance. "Are you ready?" I asked.

"Of course. It's finally time to settle things with you!" Shii declared.

I took a step toward her as soon as she was finished speaking.

"*Hraagh!*" I shouted, slashing my sword diagonally with all my strength.

"Ngh...!" She grunted, blocking the full force of the blow with her blade.

Man, she's really skilled... She'd blocked my attack without matching my strength by shifting the black sword's impact from her arms to her shoulders, her shoulders to her legs, and her legs to the ground. That was a stunt that required very precise muscle control.

"Hmm-hmm, are you surprised?" Shii asked.

"Yeah, you never cease to impress. How about this?" I responded. "First Style—Flying Shadow!" I shouted, performing a projectile slash attack while our blades were locked.

"From point-blank range?! Gah..." Shii gasped.

The ebon projectile overpowered her and sent her flying backward through the air.

This is my chance!

I pursued quickly, aiming to strike when she was vulnerable upon landing.

"Eighth Style—Eight-Span Crow!"

"You little... Don't you dare underestimate the Arkstoria name!"

Shii opened her eyes wide and perfectly deflected the eight slashes, touching her blade to each one with such grace it appeared as if she were dancing.

Something didn't feel right about that... Her movement was too precise. She reacted faster than even Shido or Idora could have. It was as if she knew exactly where my slashes would land ahead of time. *There must be a trick to this...*

I observed our surroundings and found the answer.

"Oh, that explains it...," I mumbled.

"What are you talking about?" Shii asked, cocking her head and feigning ignorance.

Geez... Is there no end to her mischief?

"That's a really clever use of water. I'm impressed," I said.

"I don't follow," she responded, continuing to play dumb.

"It's the water vapor, isn't it?"

"..."

Shii held her tongue, frustration on her face. *Bullseye.* There was a layer of thin water vapor surrounding us, and if I focused, I could sense a faint amount of Shii's spirit power within it. That meant it was a product of her ability.

"You can use this water vapor to sense the movement of my muscles, the position of my center of gravity, and the angle I swing my blade. That's how you predicted my next move and defended yourself perfectly. It's an intricate skill, one that could only be pulled off with your superior intellect and polished swordcraft. Am I right?" I asked.

"*Haah...* You're impossible, Allen. I can't believe you saw through Aqua Vision this quickly... You have me at a loss," she said with a shrug. "But just because you know what I'm doing doesn't mean you know how to counteract it. This area is under my control."

"Hmm... This might work," I responded.

I could think of one method to disrupt Shii's control of the area—brute force. I extended my ten dark tentacles into the sky and slammed them all into the schoolyard together. With an earsplitting boom, they kicked a cloud of dust into the air that absorbed the water vapor. Now she wouldn't be able to predict my movements.

"Y-you've got to be kidding me...," Shii muttered. I rushed toward her as she stood frozen in shock. "H-how are you so fast?!"

"Cherry Blossom Blade Secret Technique—Mirror Sakura Slash!" I shouted, sending eight slash attacks toward her, four on each side.

"Ngh... Gah!"

Shii used her excellent reflexes to deflect four of them and dodge three more, but the last one sliced her on the left shoulder.

"..."

She leaped backward in retreat and grimaced in pain. Her left arm hung limp at her side, forcing her to hold her sword with her right hand alone.

It doesn't look like that deep of a gash, but she's going to have trouble fighting in that state.

"Should we end this here, President?" I asked.

"...I am Shii Arkstoria, Student Council President of Thousand Blade Academy! I can't lose to a first-year from the same school!" Shii shouted, rejecting my proposal. She lifted her beautiful Soul Attire overhead. "Aqua Feast!"

Steel water flowed out of Aqua Queen to take the shape of a massive greatsword.

That thing's enormous. The sword projected tremendous waves of force; it must have contained a lot of spirit power.

"Your pure strength outclasses mine, as much as I hate to admit it. But no matter how much of a monster you are, it won't be enough to block this attack. Let's see if you're brave enough to try," Shii said.

She's obviously provoking me, but I have no choice but to go along with it. Dodging the attack would be the right call if my only goal was to win the fight. That would upset Shii, though. She wants this to go exactly her way—if it doesn't, she'll just come up with an even more harebrained scheme and challenge me again. To truly win, I need to overcome her strongest attack and defeat her in a convincing fashion.

"...Fine. I accept your challenge," I responded.

"Hmm-hmm, that's what I wanted to hear!" Shii smiled belligerently and gripped her enlarged Soul Attire. "Take this—Aqua Ark!"

She lifted her Soul Attire high into the air and produced a magnificent ark from a deluge of water rich in spirit power. A direct blow from it would knock me out instantly.

"Sixth Style—Dark Boom!" I shouted, swinging the true ebon blade as hard as I could to unleash a raging torrent of darkness. The ark and the dark slash collided violently, and the darkness consumed the ark.

"Nooo...!" Shii cried, collapsing to the ground in despair after watching Aqua Ark be wiped out so easily.

"Move, President! Now!" I yelled out in warning, but she shook her head. It seemed like she couldn't get out of the way. *Crap, what a terrible time for her to run out of spirit power!*

My tremendously powerful Dark Boom continued to race toward her as she sat there helplessly.

This is bad... A direct hit from Dark Boom could kill her in her defenseless state. Geez, she's such a handful...

I kicked hard off the ground, dashed past the projectile, and stood before her.

"Fifth Style—World Render!" I shouted, performing my strongest move—powerful enough to tear through a world—and successfully felled the torrent of darkness.

Phew, that was close...

Now that I was the last one standing in this chaotic bout, I reached out to Shii to help her off the ground.

"Are you okay, President?" I asked.

"Hee-hee, I knew you would be too nice to let me get hit!" Shii said with a vicious smile before thrusting Aqua Queen into the schoolyard. A magic circle then appeared that covered the entirety of Thousand Blade.

"What the heck?!" I exclaimed.

"Nice view, huh? You're standing right in the center of the magic circle," Shii said.

"...?!"

I didn't know what was going on, but this spot was definitely dangerous. I took a step back to escape...but wasn't fast enough.

"Too late, Allen. The shackles are already in place. You'll never escape me—Aqua Prison!" Shii yelled. Magic circles made of water appeared on my hands and feet.

What is this?! My body was so heavy it felt as if gravity had increased a hundredfold.

"Hee-hee, I've finally caught you." Shii smiled bewitchingly and rose to her feet with perfect composure. She'd only been pretending to be immobilized. "What do you think, Allen? This is Aqua Prison, the ace up my sleeve. It's a sealing art that took me a month to prepare. Now that you're caught in it, you shouldn't be able to even lift a finger," she said, puffing out her chest with pride.

She had set not one but *two* major traps for this fight. The first was the pitfall that I'd broken out of. The second was this giant magic circle. She had spent a *month* working on the latter. Competitive didn't even begin to describe her.

"This seal is certainly strong...," I responded. I performed Eight-Span Crow as a test, but could only produce three slashes.

"...Huh?" Shii gasped.

I unleashed Dark Shadow next, but my movement was sluggish.

"Y-you can still summon darkness...," she muttered.

The strange magic circles on my hands and feet dampened the effectiveness of my abilities by more than half.

"...I can't believe you can move at all. You really are inhuman," Shii said.

"Ah-ha-ha, I'll take that as a compliment," I responded.

"But it wasn't a waste! It's clear that you've been greatly encumbered! My victory is sealed!" she declared cheerfully.

"But, President... Why did you make such a risky wager? You easily could've died," I pointed out. Shii had used herself as bait to lure me to the center of the magic circle. She was lucky I was able to save her.

"Hmm-hmm, I wasn't worried. I knew you would pull through and rescue me, no matter the situation."

"You overestimate me. I'm not omnipotent."

"And yet, you *did* save me."

Shii beamed with such joy that it was hard to stay mad at her.

"*Haah*... Well, can you please never pull a stunt like that again?" I asked.

"Are you saying you won't save my life next time I'm in trouble? I'm hurt," she responded.

"No, I'll come to your aid any time you ask for my help. I just want you to avoid intentionally put yourself in danger again."

"Hee-hee, thank you." Shii gave me a dazzling smile. "Accept your fate, Allen! You can't hope to defeat me in that condition! Your unfailing kindness has cemented my victory!" she declared, taking a step forward without paying attention to her surroundings.

"S-stop!" I called out immediately.

"What? Don't yell out of nowhere like that. You scared me," Shii chided.

"Sorry about that. But I suggest you don't move from that spot."

"Why is that?"

"Look around you."

"What are you... Huh?!"

Shii's face went pale after she looked around. There was a good reason for that—she was trapped in a cage of Hazy Moons.

"When did you put those there?!" she shouted.

"I placed them when you were sitting on the ground," I answered.

"Did you catch on to how I was acting?"

"Your behavior felt a little off, so I wanted to set up some insurance."

Shii was way too tenacious to just give up like that. If she really had been out of spirit power, she would've done whatever she could to avoid getting hit directly by Dark Boom, even if it meant crawling across the ground.

"There you go being a naughty boy again. You didn't have to set nearly this many...," she muttered in annoyance, glaring at the hundreds of Hazy Moons around her. "But they're not enough to stop me. All I have to do is break through this wall of slash attacks, and victory is mine!"

"That might be true, but...I set all of these using my Soul Attire. I don't recommend trying to get through them," I warned.

"..."

Shii reached for her injured left shoulder with a grimace. I'd immobilized it with just a single strike from my black sword. So it stood to reason that hundreds of slashes from the same weapon would seriously injure her, if not kill her.

"I can use my darkness to protect you, but...that depends on what you want to do," I said kindly after picking up a small pebble.

"W-wait!" Shii cried out, going pale as she stared at the pebble.

"What is it?" I asked.

"Care to explain what you're doing, Allen?"

"Umm, I'm holding a pebble."

It was a perfectly ordinary rock I'd found on the schoolyard.

"That's not what I meant! I'm asking what you're going to do with it!"

"Ah-ha-ha, I'll leave that to your imagination."

Hazy Moon was a slash attack I could set in the air as a trap to activate as soon as anything passed through it. Throwing this pebble would trigger a slash, which would trigger another slash, and so on, leading to a tempestuous chain of attacks, with Shii at the center.

"A-are you threatening me?!" Shii asked.

"Trust me, I don't want to do this. But I'm running out of time…," I responded. I looked at my watch and saw that it was twenty minutes to eleven. Forty minutes had already passed since this ridiculous event kicked off. I wanted to check on Lia to ease my fears, and I couldn't do that until I got Shii to admit defeat.

"I didn't know you were such a bully…," Shii whined, pouting.

"I'm sorry. I'm worried about Lia and the others, so can you please make up your mind?" I urged, rolling the pebble in my hand.

She had two choices: risk serious injury by trying to break through the Hazy Moons herself or admit defeat and have me remove them. Which would she choose?

I waited as she considered her options.

"…I'll dispel Aqua Prison. Please protect me," Shii muttered after a long silence. The magic circles on my hands and feet disappeared, lifting the extra weight from my body. She had removed Aqua Prison.

"Got it. Don't move, okay? I can't guarantee your safety if you do," I warned.

I covered Shii in an exceptionally thick cloak of darkness and tossed the pebble into the air. It was shattered by a black slash, which set off a destructive storm of attacks around Shii.

"…?!"

She cowered like a frightened animal as she watched the chain of black slashes rage around her. A few of them nicked her, but the cloak of darkness protected her from injury.

"I-I'm alive…" Shii sighed with relief once all of the Hazy Moons had been activated.

"So, President. Can we consider this my victory?" I asked.

"..."

Shii bit her lower lip and nodded. She was actually admitting defeat.

"Thank you. Now, if you'll excuse me," I said.

With Shii, Lilim, and Tirith defeated, I sprinted off to find Lia.

■

As Allen fought his seniors of the Student Council, Lia was embroiled in a desperate struggle of her own.

"For goodness' sake, are you all *ever* going to give up?!" she shouted.

Fifty swordsmen stood in her way, every last one pushing themselves to keep fighting despite sporting numerous slash wounds.

"Heh-heh. We third-years are about to graduate. This is our last chance...," one of them responded.

"We're not gonna go down easy!" shouted another.

The mob was comprised of all third-year boys. Each of them had fallen for Lia during the Opening Ceremony eight months prior and had been eagerly awaiting the Crush Your Crush Competition ever since.

"Please cease this! Some of you might actually die if we continue!" Lia pleaded, pointing Fafnir at them.

"Ha-ha, you're worried about us. That just goes to show how caring you are," a boy said.

"That's one of your best aspects, but it's also a weakness... Now!" another boy yelled.

A male student leaped from the third floor of the main school building behind Lia.

"Princess Lia, I love you!" he shouted.

"Wh-what?!" She gasped.

Unlike Allen, Lia didn't do well with surprises. That was understandable, however, given the differences in their upbringing. Allen had grown up so destitute that he needed to be frugal with every candle, every grain of rice. Each day had been a struggle for survival, and in that environment, learning how to cope with the unexpected was a necessity. As a princess, Lia's childhood couldn't have been any more different. She was followed by burly guards everywhere she went, and they would take care of anything that surprised her. Consequently, she hadn't needed to learn to be adaptable.

After successfully catching Lia off guard and gaining position above her, the boy unleashed his Soul Attire. "Blinding Flash!" His sword released a tremendous light, blinding Lia momentarily.

"Ngh, Draconic Rage!" she shouted in response, scattering black and white flames about at random.

""""Gaaaaah?!""""

Though this left many of the boys seriously injured, their spirits didn't falter in the slightest.

"This isn't over! Noise Bomb!" a second student shouted, sending a transparent sphere at Lia.

"White Dragon Scales!" Lia yelled on a split-second decision, her vision still compromised. A giant shield appeared before her. The Noise Bomb crashed into the shield and exploded, assaulting her with ear-splittingly loud waves of sound.

"What's happening?!" She gasped, stumbling as the noise tore her semicircular canals and threw her off-balance.

"Time to finish this—Impact Wave!" a third boy shouted, slamming a giant hammer into the grounds of the school to shake the earth at Lia's feet.

"Ahhh!" she screamed, falling on her back due to her lack of vision and balance.

""""Got you!"""" a trio of third years shouted after their successful three-part attack. They charged toward Lia's Santa hat.

"Nooooooo!" she screamed.

"Sorry, but I can't let you have that."

Wicked darkness descended from the ceiling to crush the three boys.

""""Gah!""""

The shadowy tendrils clobbered each of them in the head, knocking them out before they even realized what happened.

"Allen...!" Lia yelled, rushing behind Allen. She had finally regained her vision.

"I'm glad you're okay, Lia," Allen said, breathing a sigh of relief after seeing that her Santa hat was still on her head. Then in an uncharacteristic display of mild anger, he readied Zeon. "You all are up against me now."

He was more than a little peeved to find fifty boys attacking Lia at once.

"A-Allen Rodol?! You've gotta be kidding... Did he defeat the entire Swordcraft Club by himself?!" a boy exclaimed.

"What about the Student Council girls?! They bragged all month about how they were gonna beat him this time. I saw how hard they worked!" another said.

"You're saying they teamed up with the Swordcraft Club and still lost?!" yet another shouted.

Paling in intimidation before Allen, the third years all took a step backward in retreat.

"Goddamn it...I'm *not* giving up Princess Lia! Not now!" one boy proclaimed.

"Don't be stupid, man! Allen's a demon! The dude doesn't have an ounce of mercy in him. He'll tear you to shreds!" another warned.

News of Allen's inhuman atrocities had reached the entirety of Thousand Blade's student body. This was just baseless gossip, of course, but these boys didn't know that. Allen had racked up a long list of incredible achievements, and the sinister quality of his darkness lent credibility to the rumors of his misdeeds.

"Oh, shut up! I've spent the last three years training tirelessly at swordcraft! This rookie first-year has no chance against me!" the first boy snapped. He charged at Allen resolutely.

"Eighth Style—Eight-Span Crow!"

"Blargh!"

Eight dark projectile slashes assaulted the boy and scattered into the night.

""""Holy crap! He's as mean as they say!""""" a few shouted.

After incapacitating the charging swordsman with astounding speed, Allen smiled softly and assumed the middle stance. "So, who's next?"

"""""…""""""

He'd practiced taking the middle stance countless times during his billion-plus years of training—there were few, if any, people in the world with a more transcendent mastery of the technique than him.

"H-his guard is perfect… We don't have a chance in hell of defeating a monster like him…," a boy said dejectedly.

"But we're never going to get another opportunity to get with Lia!" another boy insisted.

"Yeah… This is our last Crush Your Crush Competition before graduation… We can kiss our chances of becoming Princess Lia's boyfriend goodbye after this!" a third boy said.

"This may be hopeless, but we're going out with a fight! Charge!" another male student commanded.

""""Haaaaaaaa!"""""

The third-years screamed with lust in their voices and charged toward Allen…

"Dark Shadow."

…but their attempt had been doomed from the start. Allen mowed each student down with ease using his resilient darkness. Less than a minute later, all fifty third-years lay unconscious in the schoolyard.

"You're incredible, Allen… You swatted them down like flies," Lia said. She had been hiding behind him as he pummeled the boys into the dirt.

"Lia, let's go hide somewhere. I don't want anyone else to find us," Allen said.

"Okay," she responded.

They disappeared into the night and hid in the main school building.

◼

After I saved Lia from that mob of third-year boys, she and I snuck up to the roof. No one would find us here.

"This might be the most ridiculous thing they've made us do yet...," I said.

"No kidding. Thousand Blade Academy is insane...," Lia agreed.

There were still students locked in fierce battles throughout the moonlit schoolyard. A campus-wide brawl was the last thing I expected to experience on Christmas night. Were the other Elite Five Academies also holding barbaric events of their own tonight?

I glanced at the clock tower and saw that it was five minutes to eleven. The chaotic Christmas party was about to come to an end. *We had some close calls, but we'll make it out just fine if we wait here*, I thought before giving a big stretch to relieve tension.

Lia clasped her hands behind her and smiled. "Thanks, Allen."

"For what?" I responded.

"For saving me, you dummy."

"Oh. Don't mention it."

It had been my pleasure. I didn't need to be thanked for it. I just... hadn't wanted to see Lia taken by some third-years I had never even met.

We fell silent and passed the time by gazing at the stars.

"..."

"..."

"Hey, Allen," Lia said after a few minutes.

"What is it?" I responded.

"Do you...want my hat?" she asked, tugging the sleeve of my uniform and tilting her head adorably.

"Uh... W-well I, um...," I stuttered, shocked by what I'd just heard. I could feel my face growing red.

I-I do want it…

Badly. Desperately.

But would it really be okay to take it?! Wouldn't it be better to tell her my feelings on my own terms rather than rely on this silly event?!

My thoughts were racing so fast that it felt like my brain was going to fry.

"Hee-hee, I'm just joking," Lia laughed. Her smile seemed somewhat…empty.

…Lia?

I'd noticed that hollowness in her expression a lot lately. *Is something troubling her?* I racked my brains to figure out what to say to her.

"Allen… Close your eyes," she instructed.

"Huh? Why?" I asked.

"Come on… Don't you trust me?" Lia responded with upturned eyes. I couldn't possibly refuse now.

"Okay. I just have to close my eyes, right?"

I didn't know what was going on, but I went along and did as she asked,

"You can't open them no matter what, okay?" Lia insisted.

"Okay, I won't," I promised.

Ten seconds… Thirty seconds… Then a full minute passed without anything happening. Finally, something warm and soft touched my right cheek.

What was that?!

My heart started racing.

"Y-you can open your eyes now…"

I opened my eyes and saw Lia blushing slightly.

"L-L-L-Lia?! What did you just do?!" I exclaimed.

"…Tee-hee, it's a secret," she said with a mature smile. She spun away from me.

Her ears were red, but not from the cold.

Did she just…? No, I must be overthinking it! But whatever she pressed

against my cheek felt so soft… And what's more romantic than Christmas night? But that would mean…

I got lost in a tangled web of thoughts.

A few minutes later, Lia gasped. "Look, Allen! It's snowing!" she pointed out, her eyes shining as she watched white, fluffy snow fall from the sky.

"Wow, that's so pretty… It's a white Christmas," I responded.

"Yeah! Isn't it wonderful?"

The snow truly was beautiful in the moonlight.

…I'm going to keep my feelings to myself for now.

I loved Lia.

But I would only tell her my feelings when I became a swordsman worthy of a princess. I was going to do it on my own terms, without relying on an event like this.

I need to return to my practice-swing routine tomorrow for that purpose.

Lia and I shared the last hour of Christmas quietly on the rooftop.

CHAPTER 2

An Invitation & a Demon

With the chaotic Christmas party now behind us, Thousand Blade entered a short winter break. I spent my days immersed in training with Lia, Rose, and Claude.

On New Year's Eve, I went out shopping with Lia—and nearly fell flat on my face in reaction to something she told me.

"Hey, Allen. Have you heard?" she asked.

"Heard what?" I responded.

"That if you eat a bowl of soba for every year you've been alive on New Year's Eve, you're guaranteed to have good luck the next year."

I'm pretty sure that tradition is performed with soybeans, actually... It would be almost impossible to put away fifteen servings of soba...

"Let's go eat fifteen bowls each!" she exclaimed.

I hated saying no to Lia, but her suggestion was beyond what was humanly possible. For most people, anyway. But when I looked at her smile, I couldn't bring myself to refuse her outright.

"Hey, Lia. Fifteen bowls would be really hard for me, but how about this?" I began.

After some discussion, we compromised by deciding that I would have eight bowls and Lia would have twenty-two. That maintained an average of fifteen bowls of soba between us. I had no idea if there was any real point in putting myself through this… But at least it would make her happy. She celebrated joyfully and said, "We're going to have another great year!"

So I *definitely* didn't put myself through hell to wolf down eight bowls of soba for nothing. The awful indigestion and nausea I suffered afterward were worth it just to see that smile… At least that's what I convinced myself to get through it.

New Year's Day arrived.

Phew, it feels like the stomach medicine worked…, I thought, lightly rubbing my gut before putting my arms through the sleeves of the formal black suit I'd bought the other day. It was what you'd call a black lounge suit. Lia helped me buy it in a hurry after we received a letter the day after Christmas.

I can't believe this is happening…

That letter was an invitation to attend the New Year's Jubilee, which was an annual ceremony held in Liengard Palace on January 1 to celebrate the start of the new year. I had heard that the empress of Liengard herself would be there.

Why was I, of all people, invited to this? I checked the invitation multiple times thinking there must have been a mistake, but our names were clearly written on it. Lia was a Vesterian princess, so it made sense that she would be invited. But I was just a commoner. A nobody. I was clearly going to be out of place among the ambassadors and government officials from all over the continent who were going to be in attendance.

Urgh, my stomach hurts again…

It was starting to seem like these stomachaches were triggered by stress.

Do I have to go…?

I sighed loudly just as I heard a knock on my door.

"Are you done changing, Allen?" Lia asked.

"Yeah, I just finished," I answered.

Chapter 2

Lia walked in wearing a long-sleeved kimono.

"That suit looks perfect on you!" she said with a smile after studying my outfit closely from top to bottom.

"…Oh, th-thanks," I responded a little belatedly, stunned at the sight of Lia's outfit.

The kimono was red and refined. A golden sash was wrapped around her slim waist, and the area of the garment between the sleeves and the bodice was decorated with gorgeous flower embroidery. Her hair had been elegantly styled, held in place with a wine-red hairpin shaped like a flower. The increased maturity of her look took my breath away.

"Hmm-hmm, are you enchanted by my beauty?" Lia asked jokingly.

"Yeah, you look stunning," I responded, accidentally sharing exactly what I was thinking.

"O-oh yeah? Thanks…"

"Y-you're welcome…"

We both stammered awkwardly and blushed.

"…"

"…"

Lia and I struggled to break the silence, glancing at each other and looking away whenever we happened to meet eyes. I looked at my watch and saw that it was nine in the morning. The New Year's Jubilee began at ten, so we didn't have much time.

"W-we should get going. It starts in an hour," I said.

"Yeah, good thinking!" Lia responded.

Still feeling awkward, we headed for Liengard Palace.

■

The palace was a surprisingly short walk from the Thousand Blade dorms. We went through simple registration at the front gate, then stepped inside the residence of Liengard's empress. The expansive entrance hall, which was being used as the venue for the ceremony, was so extravagant that it felt like we had stumbled into another world.

"This is amazing...," I muttered as I looked around.

The latest LCD screens hung on the pillars. Giant, imposing clay sculptures stood in the corners. Famous paintings decorated the walls. Large plates were stacked with enough delicious food to feed a village for weeks.

The décor is all over the place... The luxury of the venue was overwhelming, and there was no unity or consistency to the presentation. It was just as Lia said on the way here—national ceremonies like the New Year's Jubilee were primarily held to invite foreign guests and flaunt the country's prestige.

I continued to gaze at the otherworldly hall until I heard Shii's voice from behind me.

"Oh, hey Lia. Hello, Rodol," she said.

...Rodol? What's this about? Feeling weirded out by the stiffness of her address, I turned around to find Shii in a gorgeous long-sleeved kimono.

"Happy New Year, President," I responded.

"Happy New Year, Shii. That kimono is really pretty!" Lia complimented her.

"Happy New Year to you too... Hee-hee, your kimono is beautiful as well, Lia," Shii said with a gentle smile.

I didn't expect to run into Shii here...though I guess I should have. She was a member of the famous Arkstoria family, which had held important positions in the Liengard government for generations. The New Year's Jubilee was probably an annual thing for her.

"I came to a realization after the Christmas party," Shii said. Though her lips were still curled into a gentle smile, she was staring daggers at me.

The President's really mad, isn't she...? She was talking to me like she barely knew me. It was as clear as day that I'd somehow offended her.

"U-umm... What was it?" I asked. I had a bad feeling about this.

"That you're a pervert who likes to bully girls."

"Huh..."

It was the first day of the new year, and she was already giving me hell.

"I could see it on your face at that moment. You were having the time of your life messing with me," Shii said in an accusatory tone. She must have been talking about when I'd picked up the pebble and made her choose between continuing to fight or surrendering.

"I-I'm sorry you took it that way, but I wasn't trying to mess with you," I assured her. I'd set that trap and forced Shii to give in because I was worried sick about Lia's Santa hat getting taken before I reached her. I had zero ill intentions.

"Hmph, like I'd believe that... This was the second, no, the third time you've taken delight in bullying me," Shii said.

"Huh? What are you talking about?" I asked.

"The first time was when you embarrassed me during the Club Budget War. The second was when you cheated at poker and gave yourself a full house. Don't tell me you forgot about those incidents."

"Uhh..."

Oh yeah... So much has happened over the past year that I really did forget those two things ever happened.

"Anyway, I'm going to continue to treat you like a stranger until you change your ways!" Shii declared, turning away from me.

She's so childish... The President loved to pass herself off as a big-sister figure, but the way she pouted just made her look like a little kid. *I'm at a loss here...* She could get really annoying when she was upset, and it took a lot of effort to get back on her good side. And then she would get arrogant once I did, too.

I smiled awkwardly, but was saved from having to respond when a man came up behind her.

"What do you think you're doing, Shii?" he asked.

"G-go away, Father!" Shii commanded.

So this was her father, Rodis Arkstoria. He was about 180 centimeters tall, and the white streaks in his black hair suggested he was around forty years old. He looked as tough as any man I'd ever seen—he wasn't muscular, but he had a well-balanced build, and his hawk-like eyes, the scar on his left eyelid, and his fine black beard gave him an imposing air. His long white kimono, gray *hakama*, and dark yellow-green coat suited him well.

"...I see. You must be the Allen Rodol I've heard so much about," he said, glancing at me. He ignored his daughter and approached me. "I am Rodis Arkstoria, Shii's father—though I'm sure you already put that much together. I serve as... Well, I suppose my job title isn't important. I have something I need to tell you, boy."

"Wh-what is it?" I asked.

He waited three long seconds before responding. "My daughter's off-limits."

"...Huh?"

"Don't play the fool. I've known for some time about your...unusual relationship with her."

"Uh... What?"

The heck does he mean by 'unusual'? I searched in vain for a proper response until Rodis grit his teeth and started trembling.

"You are all my daughter talks about anymore. It's Allen this, Allen that... And she always has this grin on her face when she brings you up..."

"F-Father! What are you saying?!" Shii yelled, blushing furiously and shaking her dad by the shoulders. That did nothing to stop him.

"Weren't you just saying you were going to ask him out?" Rodis asked.

"WH-WH-WHAT?!" Shii shouted as loudly as she could before covering his mouth. Her ears were so red it seemed like they would burst into flames. "M-my father was making all of that up, Allen! I never said anything like that!"

"H-huh...," I responded.

"Anyway, I'll see you at school! Let's go, Father!" Shii said, pushing Rodis away into the crowd of people.

"I never thought I'd meet another dad who was as much of a helicopter parent as mine...," Lia said.

She was right—Rodis seemed nearly as protective of Shii as Gris Vesteria was of Lia. *I'll bet all dads are like that with their daughters.*

I took a breath and looked around the hall. *The variety of people here is something to behold.* I saw people in warrior garb, people wearing tricolor dresses who were clearly from abroad, and people in giant white hats favored by hunter tribes to the south. The range of outfits gave the event quite an exotic flair.

As I inspected the guests, I caught sight of someone in a particularly flamboyant outfit.

"Is that Clown?" I asked Lia.

"Where? Oh, it really is him," she replied.

I had spotted Clown Jester, the manager of the Holy Knights Association's Aurest branch. He was chatting with someone.

Man, it takes guts to dress like that at this kind of event... There was no dress code, but I couldn't believe he decided to show up to the New Year's Jubilee wearing his usual harlequin getup. The empress was going to be here... Clown was the definition of a free spirit.

"We should go say hello," I said.

"Wait. Look at who he's talking to," Lia responded, turning serious.

"Huh?"

I looked next to Clown and saw Rize, wearing her usual red kimono.

"I feel bad not going right away, but let's wait until later to greet him. We shouldn't go anywhere near the Blood Fox...," Lia insisted, shaking her head.

Chairwoman Reia had dissuaded us from associating with Rize, who had a terrible reputation. *She's actually a really good person, though...* I scratched my cheek, unsure of what to do.

"Oh, if it isnae Allen!"

Rize noticed me and walked over, bringing Clown with her.

"Crap, she found us...," Lia muttered, grimacing openly. She always wore her emotions on her sleeve.

"Hello, Ms. Rize and Mr. Clown. Happy New Year," I said.

"...Happy New Year," Lia followed begrudgingly. The two adults responded in kind.

"I dinnae expect to see you on the first day of the year, Allen. This is going tae be a good year indeed," Rize said cheerfully, inspecting me with her narrow eyes.

"Ah-ha-ha, I'm very happy to see you too," I responded.

"R-really? Ye're too kind." She hid her mouth with her fan and waved her right hand in protest.

Clown spoke up next, sounding as casual as ever. "Oh, Rize... What are you doing taking him seriously? He's obviously just trying to butter you—GRK!" He stopped speaking and clutched his chest in pain.

"M-Mr. Clown?!" I shouted.

"Are you okay?!" Lia entreated.

Pale in the face, he shook his head and grabbed Rize's sleeve. I didn't know why, but it seemed like he couldn't breathe.

"Ye know what they say, Clown. If ye cannae say anythin' nice, say nothin' at all... Take care, now," Rize said frigidly. He nodded vigorously.

"Pfaah! *Haah, haah*... Ah-ha-ha, you're as cruel as ever...," Clown managed as he gasped for breath. It seemed like Rize had released him from some power.

"Hee-hee, I have tae be. Though I must admit, that acting wasnae unimpressive, Clown."

"...You could tell I was acting?"

"Naturally. Being unable tae breathe would hardly faze you."

Actually, I think not being able to breathe would be life-threatening for anyone…, I internally objected. Clown seemed just as formidable as Rize.

"How would you grade my performance? I thought that was pretty convincing, myself," Clown asked.

"Hmm. I give ye three points," Rize responded.

"Out of five?"

"No, out of a thousand."

"Man, you're harsh."

They laughed together. These two were really, uh…unique people. I had the feeling they went way back.

This just confuses me even more, though. If that was Rize's Soul Attire just now, then that's the second time I've seen her use it—the first was at the Unity Festival—but I'm still just as clueless about what it actually does.

Rize checked the clock in the hall and gave Clown a look.

"Anyway, that's all the time I have. If ye'll excuse me," she said with a wave of her fan.

"Oh, are you already leaving?" I asked.

The New Year's Jubilee was just getting underway. Did she have plans after this?

"I've already greeted Her Majesty, and I must prepare fae my next business meeting. It's time I get goin'," she explained, waving.

"I have an important meeting at the Aurest branch, so I'll be heading out, too," Clown said with a slight bow.

"Okay. Good luck with work," I responded.

"Hee-hee, thanks," Rize said.

"Thanks a lot," Clown replied.

Lia waited until the two left Liengard Palace to speak. She had been silent for the entire conversation.

"They sure have guts prioritizing work over a ceremony the empress is attending…," she said.

"Ah-ha-ha, that's just like them," I replied.

Just then, a stunningly beautiful girl walked toward us followed by a crowd of guards.

I see her in the newspaper all the time... That must be Wendy Liengard.

Wendy Liengard was the empress who ruled over this country. She had bright pink hair that reached her back. She was about 165 centimeters tall, and appeared to be around fifteen, the same age as me. Her round eyes and tender lips made her seem as kind and gorgeous as an angel. She also boasted a flawless figure—long and slender limbs, a large chest, and a slim waist. Tonight, she was clad in an elegant white dress with pink accents that exposed her collarbone.

She had inherited her title at just ten years of age. When you factored that in with her superior intellect and ingenuity, there was little wonder why she was said to be the most gifted girl in Liengard.

"Wow... Are you Allen Rodol?" the empress asked.

"Y-yes, Your Majesty...," I responded.

"Tee-hee. Please, there's no need to be so formal. The New Year's Jubilee is a time for celebration," she said.

"Th-thank you," I stammered.

After that brief exchange, Lia turned toward the empress. "I'm Lia Vesteria, First Princess of Vesteria. Thank you very much for your kind invitation, Your Majesty," she greeted the empress with all the elegance of a princess.

"I'm Wendy Liengard, empress of Liengard. I am pleased to see you accepted my invitation," the empress responded. She turned back at me. "Would you be willing to speak in private, Mr. Rodol?"

I couldn't believe my ears.

Why me...?

I didn't have the faintest idea what the empress of Liengard would have to talk about with a commoner like me. That said, I could hardly refuse a request from the ruler of the country.

"Yes, of course," I responded.

"I'm glad to hear it," the empress said with a radiant smile. She looked at Lia apologetically. "My apologies, Princess Lia, but do you mind if I borrow Mr. Rodol for a bit?"

"N-no, I don't mind...," Lia responded reluctantly. She was yet to inherit the throne from her father, which meant the empress was above her. She was in no position to refuse her request.

"I'll be right back when we're done, Lia," I assured her.

"...Okay," she said.

I left Lia, who looked uneasy, and followed the empress to the second floor of Liengard Palace.

■

A great many people watched us with curiosity as we passed.

"H-hey, look over there! Her Majesty is walking alone with a guy! She doesn't even have any guards with her!"

"Wait a minute, that's Allen Rodol!"

"Really? I've heard he's gotten involved with some dark business lately. Rumor has it he has a close connection to the Blood Fox."

"He's got ties to Rize at his age?! He must be quite the charmer..."

"I would avoid him if I were you..."

I can hear everything you're saying... The bad rumors about me had apparently spread beyond swordcraft academies and into high society. *Do things always have to work out this way?* I thought, sighing mentally so that no one would hear me.

We snaked through the corridors of Liengard Palace, only stopping when we climbed a staircase and reached a room at the end of a hallway.

"Okay, Mr. Rodol. I apologize for the modest furnishings, but please enter," she said, opening the door for me to walk through.

"Thank you," I responded, and walked in.

It was a perfectly ordinary guest room furnished with only the essentials: a dresser, a bed, and a desk.

"What are we doing here, Your Ma—," I started to say, stopping when I heard the door lock. *Huh? Did she just trap me in here? This can't be good.* "Your Majesty?"

"Tee-hee, we can finally speak alone, Allen Rodol," the empress said after securing the entrance. She smiled alluringly and sat on the bed. "Come on, don't just stand there. Make yourself comfortable." She patted the spot next to her.

"O-okay…"

I walked to the bed while inconspicuously inspecting the chamber. *There's one person behind the hanging scroll, two people in the closet, and one person behind the window curtain.* I could hear them breathing when I listened closely. They were probably guards. *She must be taking precautionary measures, as an empress should.*

"Excuse me," I said, sitting down about a meter away to her right.

"You're surprisingly uncomfortable around girls for someone who lives under the same roof as a Vesterian princess," the empress said, smiling sadistically. She slid her hips toward mine, filling the space I'd been careful to leave.

Why's she sitting so close to me?! And man, her skin is soft!

She placed her soft thigh on my right hand, closing in enough for her pleasant scent to reach my nose.

C-calm down… Wait, how does she know that I'm living with Lia?!

I took a deep breath to slow my quickening heartbeat and my racing thoughts. I heard the empress giggle with satisfaction; she was closely observing me.

"Tell me about yourself, Allen. I've heard the rumors, but I want to hear things straight from your mouth," she said, poking my cheek.

"Sorry to answer your question with a question, but why do you want to know about me?"

I had no idea why a person of her vaunted status would take interest in a nobody like me.

"Hmm… It started as simple curiosity, I guess," she answered.

"Really? Why?"

"You realize how famous you are, right? There are so many rumors about you, each worse than the last. Some say you're a swordsman of darkness who rules Thousand Blade Academy, others say you're a fiend who is plotting to overthrow the government, and yet more claim you're a spy for the Black Organization. It's quite amusing, really. How could I resist investigating after hearing all that?"

"I-I see..."

So the stories about me had even reached the empress.

"But each tale ended up being completely out of pace with reality. You're nothing but an ordinary swordcraft academy student."

"Yeah, that's ri—"

"At least, that's what I was supposed to think."

"...Huh?"

A spark formed in the empress's eyes as her speculation went off the rails.

"I don't know who it is, but someone is making every effort to manipulate information around you. They're making sure you come off as exceptional, but not so much that you draw unwanted attention. At the same time, they're spreading lies to harm your reputation and ensure that anyone who investigates will conclude that you're perfectly unremarkable."

She smiled confidently, sounding like a conspiracy theorist.

"My guess is that they're doing this so that you reach your potential without catching the attention of the Four Imperial Knights—the highest-ranking members of the Thirteen Oracle Knights—or the Seven Holy Blades of the Holy Knights Association. I'm almost convinced they're doing this so you can spread your wings and fly into the world when you're ready."

"U-uhh..."

I had no idea where to even begin to correct her. I'd learned something today—a smart person coming to a big misunderstanding led to nothing but trouble.

"Anyway, I have a few things I want to ask. Is that okay with you?" the empress asked.

"Yes, of course," I responded with a nod. Her first question was surprisingly simple.

"First, where are you from?"

"Goza Village. It's pretty far from Aurest."

"Goza Village, you said? So you're not from Liengard?"

"No, I am. It's a poor, run-of-the-mill hamlet, but it's in Liengard."

Maybe the empress didn't know about Goza Village because its economic footprint was so small.

"Huh… Need I remind you that I am the empress of Liengard? I know of every municipality within my domain, so I can declare with confidence that there is no place known as Goza Village in this country."

"…What?"

Goza Village…didn't exist? That was ludicrous.

"I-I promise you it's real! The village is northwest of Grand Swordcraft Academy. It's a long journey, but you can't miss it," I insisted.

"What are you saying? There's nothing to the northwest of Grand Swordcraft Academy but a barren wasteland. That's been the case for decades," the empress said.

"…Huh?"

Goza Village was a rich agricultural community where fields stretched out in all directions. It was also in close proximity to a stream abundant with fish. Mom and Ol' Bamboo lived there, and everyone in town worked to support each other.

And she's saying there's a wasteland there? That's impossible.

This had to be some sort of misunderstanding.

"That's pretty strange… I couldn't find anyone named Allen Rodol on the census. Were you born abroad?" the empress asked.

"N-no, there's no way," I answered, unsettled. The absurdity of her questions had me at a loss for words.

"Oh, you're keeping that a secret, too? Fine, next question."

"H-huh…"

This conversation wasn't sitting right with me, but I answered her questions anyway. She inquired about my favorite foods, my hobbies, my dreams for the future, and other things you would ask when first meeting someone.

What's the meaning of this?

I answered question after question, and before I knew it, she had asked ten in total.

"Umm, Your Majesty? Why are you asking me these—"

"All right, the requirements have been met. Prepare to become my servant!" the empress commanded before pushing me down onto the bed.

"Wh-what are you doing?!" I shouted.

"Hee-hee, here's the thing about me. When I see a young, promising, and pure guy like you, I just can't help myself…" She mounted my stomach and smiled sadistically. "Ooo, you're so firm and muscular… And now that body of yours is all mine." She traced my chest with a long, slim finger.

"S-stop joking around!" I pleaded, twisting to try to throw her off me to no avail.

"Engrave—Love Slave!" the empress yelled, summoning her Soul Attire. It took the form of a long nail on her index finger.

What's going on here?! I didn't know what she was trying to do, but I had to put a stop to it.

"…Your Majesty. Releasing your Soul Attire is no laughing matter. You're going to force me to defend myself," I warned.

"Aww, you're so cute when you act tough," the empress purred.

"With all due respect, do you really think that's sharp enough to stab me?"

"Of course. Reputation says you're monstrously strong, but you're defenseless in this position. And I may not look it, but I'm quite skilled with a sword... Hah!"

She plunged Love Slave down toward my chest. *Man, she's fast.* She wasn't lying about being skilled in swordcraft. But she was going to need a sharper blade than that to cut through my cloak of darkness.

"Hah!" I shouted, covering my body in shadows to perfectly block the attack.

"Ahh!" she cried when the tip of her Soul Attire touched the darkness, grimacing in pain.

"S-sorry! Are you okay?!" I asked.

"Just kidding," she said before thrusting her finger at my chest again.

"Wha?!"

She sliced my skin, leaving a cut that bled slightly.

What's happening?!

Something like her consciousness entered my mind.

"Th-this feeling... Is this a mental manipulation Soul Attire?!" I asked.

"Ding ding, correct! Love Slave enables me to engrave proof of enslavement into a person's body after I get them to answer ten questions. The requirements for activating it are quite strict, but once I assert my dominance over a target, the effect is absolute. You are my servant from this day forward," the empress explained.

"..."

The strength drained from my body. I lost control of the darkness, and my mind was starting to fade. This was...really bad.

"Don't worry, my sweet Allen. You have nothing to fear. In just a moment, you won't be able to think of anything other than me," the empress whispered in my ear after hugging me tight.

Crap..., I thought as my consciousness faded.

What gives you the right to invade my world, bitch?!

Then I heard *him*, sounding very offended.

"What the... Ahh?!" the empress screamed as her Soul Attire shattered, and she tumbled out of bed. Her four guards jumped out of their hiding places at once.

"What dreadful malice..."

"How dare you harm Her Majesty!"

"Looks like the stories about you were true!"

"Repent for your crime with your life, scoundrel!"

The guards all swung their Soul Attires at me with incredible speed. They were probably senior holy knights in the employ of the government. They had to be skilled to be entrusted with protecting the empress.

I'm...in trouble...

I wasn't yet free of Love Slave's influence. My vision was flickering, I could barely think, and my legs were shaky. The situation couldn't have been worse.

"Ngh..."

Stumbling this way and that, I somehow forced myself to my feet.

""""Die!""""

The guards slashed at me from all sides.

I can't dodge them. I don't have time to draw my sword, either. Maybe I can at least summon the cloak of darkness, I thought, but when I tried to do so, my body performed Dark Shadow instead.

""""Huh?!""""

Dark tentacles shot out and moved of their own accord, pulverizing the guards' Soul Attires and piercing their abdomens in less than a second.

"Gahhh!"

"What was that...?!"

"How did he defeat us...so fast...?"

"Impossible..."

The guards slunk to the floor after having their Soul Attires shattered. Though they weren't dead, they would succumb to their wounds if left untreated.

Wh-where did this strength come from?! Dark Shadow had become significantly more destructive. *There's no doubt about it. That move was from* him.

I gulped, overwhelmed by the bloodshed—and then the gloom sprang to life again. The tendrils bent back, ready to crack forward like whips and finish off the dying guards.

"Stop!" I screamed, focusing as hard as I could to sever my Spirit Core's interference—and was relieved to find the darkness dispelled, and the strong malice gone from my mind.

Th-that was close…

It seemed like Chairwoman Reia was right; my Spirit Core couldn't control me when my mind was clear.

I need to hurry and heal those guards. The unconscious men had lost a lot of blood. By the looks of it, they would die in about a minute if I didn't do something. I sent healing darkness toward their abdomens.

"""""Urgh…"""""

The gloom quickly closed their wounds, healing them completely. They were still unconscious, but they would surely wake soon.

This could've ended up a lot worse…

The empress wielded a mental manipulation–type Soul Attire. Her victory was all but assured once the requirements for its activation were met, which made the skill incredibly dangerous. But in the process of altering my mind, she'd accidentally reached into the Soul World where *he* slumbered…and this was the result.

Man, this looks horrible… I looked around and saw nothing but black. My darkness had stained the dresser, the bed, the walls, and the ceiling, giving the room the appearance of an endless void. Evidently, my Spirit Core had been very offended by the empress's reckless attempt to enter his world. I felt a hair-raising malice emanating from the sludge-like gloom he'd spewed.

"Wh-why won't this open?!" the empress cried, desperately turning the doorknob. Her face was pale.

That's not gonna budge... Darkness clung densely to the door, conforming to the wall around it. It would probably be faster to just smash through the wall.

"Someone save me! Please!" she wailed, pounding on the pitch-black door. The empress looked like she was having a panic attack. Her right hand was wounded, and fresh blood spilled from it every time she struck the door. *His* darkness was still dangerous, even after it was separated from my body.

I need to get her to calm down first. I addressed her as gently as I could. "Please calm down, Your Majesty. There is nothing to fear."

"S-stay away from me...," the empress stammered. She shook her head and collapsed to the floor. She was truly terrified. I decided to keep my distance so as not to agitate her further.

"Understood. I won't move from this spot. But will you let me heal you, at least? Your wounds will get infected," I requested. I slowly reached my healing gloom toward her injured hand.

"No, stop... I'm so sorry, I shouldn't have attacked you like that... Please spare my life...," she pleaded, tears in her eyes.

She's probably traumatized by his *darkness...* Where had that bold attitude of hers gone? I was surprised at how easily she'd been rattled.

What should I do...? I wondered, scratching my cheek.

"Your Majesty, we heard screaming!"

"Are you okay?! Please respond!"

I heard multiple men outside the room, probably senior holy knights who'd rushed here after hearing the commotion. It was then that I realized the dire situation I was in.

Oh crap... I'm in severe danger, aren't I? The room was stained pitch-black, the four guards were unconscious and bloodied, and the empress was crying and begging for mercy. *The circumstantial evidence will make me look like a dangerous criminal...*

I would be finished as soon as the guards entered the room. There was no chance the empress would tell them the true story; she would command them to arrest me right on the spot. I would be branded as a traitor and given the death penalty.

This is seriously bad.

I felt the blood drain from my face. I could proclaim my innocence for all the world to hear, but no one would believe a commoner from a village no one had even heard of over the empress. It was plain as day whose testimony a courtroom would side with.

What should I do?! I thought, feeling seriously stressed. A moment later, I heard a giant explosion outside the room, followed by many screams.

Wh-what was that?!

An explosion in Liengard Palace, the residence of the empress, would send the place into a state of crisis.

Is it the Black Organization?! They had been doggedly pursuing Lia—or more specifically, the eidolon residing within her. It was a likely possibility.

Hold on. I'm worried about what's happening outside, but I have a more pressing matter to attend to first..., I thought, looking at the empress. She was still on the floor, shaking like a frightened animal and staring at me. She wasn't even paying attention to what was happening outside.

The empress won't listen to me if she's this scared. I need to correct her misunderstanding about my darkness first. I slowly drew my sword and used it to cut the palm of my left hand. Blood trickled from the painful cut.

"Wh-what are you doing...?" she asked.

"Please watch closely, Your Majesty," I instructed. I focused gloom into my right index finger and slowly slid it over the cut on my left hand. The substance's healing powers closed the cut immediately.

"No way... I've heard rumors, but is that really a healing Soul Attire?! Its power feels so brutal, so sinister!"

"Yes, it is. I know it looks frightening, but it's really quite gentle."

It wasn't actually a healing Soul Attire; that was just a white lie to get her to calm down. The thing was, healing Soul Attire had a reputation for not being dangerous.

"I can heal your injuries as well, if you'll allow it," I offered. She held out her bruised and bleeding right hand, still trembling. At the very least, it looked like I had gotten her to drop her guard a bit. "Thank you, Your Majesty. I'm going to heal you now."

I reached my darkness toward her hand.

"…" She opened her eyes a few seconds later to see her hand restored to its original beauty. "…That stuff was so warm. It was totally different from before."

"Oh, sorry about that. That last kind of darkness…has given me a lot of headaches," I said jokingly.

The empress giggled. "Tee-hee, what do you mean? It's your power."

"I still have trouble controlling it. I'm a Reject Swordsman, you see."

"Reject Swordsman… Oh yeah, I remember coming across bogus intelligence about that. I heard that you were so inept that none of your instructors would accept you into their school of swordcraft…"

"Th-that's not a good memory of mine…" I really didn't want to talk about that.

Okay, I think now's the time. That exchange should have lessened her fear of the darkness. I probably didn't have long before the guards broke in, so I needed to bring this up now.

"Anyway… How about we sweep what just happened under the rug?" I proposed. I thought that was fair.

The empress looked stunned. "Y-you're forgiving me? After what I just did to you?"

"Yes, I am. I'm fine with leaving it at that."

The empress had tried to pull off something pretty disgusting. But her attempt failed, and I wasn't harmed, so ultimately I wouldn't hold it against her.

"So we can pretend it never happened? You won't…scare me like that again?" she asked.

"Yes, of course," I assured her.

"Thank goodness…" She clasped her hands before her chest and sighed with relief.

"I have one condition, though—please don't tell anyone I attacked your guards."

"That's fine with me. I forgive you for that transgression," she said, standing up and reassuming her haughty attitude. It seemed like she had decided I wasn't a threat.

"Thank you very much," I responded with a slight bow, feeling relieved.

Thank goodness… That was one of the biggest crises I'd faced in my entire life. To be honest, I wasn't that skilled at conversation; in fact, I would even go so far as to say I was below average. It was a miracle I'd been able to talk her down.

Just when I resolved things with the empress, the holy knights finally broke down the darkness-sealed door.

""""Your Majesty, are you okay?!"""""

The swordsmen charged in together, holding their Soul Attires.

"Rhody, Gonso, Evans, Torys?!" One of them gasped.

"Damn it… Did you kill them?!" another shouted at me.

The holy knights looked at their bloodied and unconscious comrades and glared at me with animosity.

"Stand down. You would stand no chance against him in a fight. They are only unconscious, and the situation is under control," the empress said, calming the guards. "More importantly, what was that explosion? What's happening out there?"

One of the guards hurriedly gave a report. "I-I see… Yes, Your Majesty. We have received a video message from the Holy Ronelian Empire! It is playing on the LCD screens on the first floor. Please follow us!"

"The Holy Ronelian Empire... I doubt what they have to say is pleasant," the empress said.

The Holy Ronelian Empire was a nefarious superpower that was constantly at odds with the Five Powers. According to the Holy Knights Association, the empire secretly ran the Black Organization.

"Mr. Rodol, would you mind coming with me?" the empress asked.

"No, not at all," I responded.

The empress and I walked to the first floor of Liengard Palace, where we found a large crowd of senior holy knights.

"Allen!"

Lia ran toward me as soon as she spotted me.

"I'm glad you're okay, Lia!" I responded.

"You too, Allen...! Huh?" She looked relieved at first, but then she froze. "Do you mind?" Lia asked as she leaned forward to sniff me.

"Wh-what is it?" I asked.

"...Allen, you smell like the empress. Care to explain?"

"?!"

The empress's scent must have been gotten on me when she pushed me onto the bed.

"U-um, well...," I stammered.

"Go on," Lia said, tilting her head. Her kind smile didn't reach her eyes.

What should I say?! Giving her the truth would necessitate telling her that the empress attacked me... I don't want to say that where someone could overhear us, and it would upset Lia, too.

At a loss for how to answer, I decided to evade her question with a terrible excuse. "B-because the empress is wearing perfume. Some of it probably got on me."

"...Hmm. Interesting," Lia muttered, glaring at me. She didn't seem convinced.

Shortly afterward, the senior holy knights prostrated themselves before the empress.

""""Thank goodness you're safe, Your Majesty!"""

"I appreciate the concern. I am glad to see you all are unhurt too. Can you explain the situation, Rodis?" the empress asked, turning to her trusted confidant.

"Three bombs that were planted on the first floor of the palace exploded simultaneously. Fortunately, the blazes have already been extinguished. Five people were injured, but they're being treated with healing Soul Attires. And…please look over there," Rodis responded, giving a concise report. He pointed to a giant LCD screen on the wall, which was displaying the Holy Ronelian flag, along with a timer with fifty-eight seconds remaining. "That's a video message from the Holy Ronelian Empire. It's only showing a timer at the moment, but a mechanical voice spoke when the countdown started."

"What did it say?"

"Three things. First, that the message was from the emperor of the Holy Ronelian Empire. Second, that the message would begin in five minutes, and that he wanted us to bring you here before then. And finally, that he had prepared gifts for us. We believe those were the explosives. What should we do, Your Majesty?" Rodis asked, waiting for the empress's orders.

"Hmm… Let's listen to the Ronelian emperor's message first. We can decide our course of action after that."

"Understood."

We waited as the timer counted down, and once it reached zero, a mechanical voice spoke through the screen.

"That's exactly five minutes. Have the leaders of the Five Powers gathered? I introduced myself at the beginning of the broadcast, but I'll do so again. I am Barel Ronelia, the emperor of the Holy Ronelian Empire."

So Barel Ronelia was delivering the message directly. I'd heard that he had never shown himself in public because he hated the attention. He always used this mechanical voice when addressing other nations.

Barel wants the leaders of the Five Powers to hear this. That meant his message was relevant to the Five Powers as a whole, not just Liengard.

"I have much I would like to talk to you about, but I know how busy we all are, so I'll get straight to the point." Barel cleared his throat before continuing. "The Holy Ronelian Empire has entered a treaty of friendship with five demons."

""""What?!""""

Lia, the empress, Shii, Rodis, and nearly everyone else in the room turned pale.

"...What's a demon?" I asked, totally out of the loop.

"Demons are a superior species of monster with highly developed intelligence and fearsome strength. They're the enemy of humanity. No one knows where they come from or why they're so hostile toward us. Only three have ever been seen, and according to history, the Seven Holy Blades who faced them had to make great sacrifices to defeat them," Lia explained.

"Yikes, they sound dangerous..."

An alliance between the Holy Empire and a group of demons definitely sounded like trouble.

"Though I suppose, 'treaty of friendship' makes it sound grander than it is. We're simply cooperating for now because our interests are aligned. I suspect we're on thin ice. Anyway, you should be receiving our present in a matter of seconds... I hope you enjoy it," Barel said just as the upper floors of Liengard Palace were literally blasted away.

""""AHHHHH?!""""

The guests of honor screamed, panicking as an avalanche of rubble fell upon us. This was accompanied by violent gales, which kicked up clouds of dust that obscured our surroundings.

What's going on?! I thought. I whipped out my sword to cut down the rubble falling toward me. Lia, Shii, and the senior holy knights did the same.

"Lia, don't leave my side!" I shouted.

"Okay!" she responded.

The dust cloud eventually cleared to reveal a winged man. He looked down at us from above as he calmly flapped his wings.

"Now this is a surprise. Some of you have a decent amount of spirit power despite being of the inferior race," he said, not hiding the contempt in his eyes. "Greetings, you lowly, unenlightened humans. I am the proud demon Seele Grazalio, and I have entered your filthy domain in search of someone."

Seele Grazalio had handsome features and straight black hair. He stood at around 190 centimeters tall and had the look of someone in their mid-twenties. He wore a well-fitted tailcoat, and appeared almost entirely human, save for his narrow, crimson eyes and sinister, dark purple wings. His demeanor was so aloof that it was clear at a glance he wasn't human.

As the mass panic continued, the empress stepped up and spoke for everyone present.

"Greetings, Mr. Grazalio. I am Wendy Liengard, the empress of Liengard. Would you be willing to talk?" she asked.

"*I have nothing to say to a member of your inferior race*—that's how most demons would respond. But fine… I am an open-minded man. I'll give you ten seconds of my time. Put that pathetic brain of yours to work and use it wisely," Seele responded.

"Thank you very much. You said you were looking for someone. Could you give me their name?"

"What would be the point in telling you?"

"I am the ruler of Liengard. No one has more thorough knowledge of this land than me. I believe I could assist you in your search."

The empress smiled kindly as she offered her assistance. She had to be trying to avoid direct combat with the demon.

"Pfft… Ha-ha-ha!" Seele grabbed his stomach and bellowed with laughter. "You think a dirty little creature like you could be of help to

a noble demon? I wondered where you were going with that... Know your place, human!" he yelled ferociously.

The empress was unfazed by his intense malice. "Did you not just join forces with Emperor Barel of Ronelia?"

"...Hmph, he's a special case. He's the king of your inferior race, and his transcendent strength far surpasses your usual limitations."

It seemed like Barel Ronelia had somehow earned the demons' respect.

"Do you intend to search all of Liengard by yourself, Mr. Grazalio? That sounds like a difficult task..."

"Hah, do not measure me by human standards. With my demonic might, I won't even need a day to search every corner of this puny country!" Seele said with a sneer. He clearly had no intention of changing his abusive attitude.

The empress's guards watched in silence, clenching their fists so tightly they started to bleed. Clearly, it was taking everything they had to retain their composure in the face of their sovereign being insulted.

"I grow bored of talking. I'm going to give you a choice," Seele said. He drew his sword and smiled maliciously.

The empress sighed loudly. Her attempt at negotiation had failed. "*Haah*... I knew there would be no point in trying to reason with an *unenlightened* demon."

"...What did you just say?"

"My apologies, but I have had enough of this conversation. Do it now."

""""Gravity Square!"""" four deep voices shouted, summoning four giant green boards that closed in on Seele from all sides.

"Ngh...?!" he grunted.

Four senior holy knights had taken position in the corners of the hall and unleashed a restraining spell with perfect timing. I didn't know when they could've possibly coordinated that with the empress.

"A gravity ability, huh...? Is this really all the strength you could manage with four people?!" Seele shouted, trying to break out of the gravity spell.

"""Water Jail!""" another group of senior holy knights shouted, stopping him with a clear sphere of water.

"What?!" Seele gasped, completely immobilized by the gravity boards and Water Jail.

Rodis jumped up behind the demon with his sword raised. "You're dead!"

He and the holy knights' chain attack was perfectly coordinated; they must have practiced this maneuver countless times.

Incredible... I can see why these senior holy knights were entrusted with protecting government personnel! I thought.

Unfazed at being back into a corner, Seele looked at Rodis as if he were an insect. "Execration—Fire Torture!" he yelled.

"Whuh?!" Rodis lost his balance and tumbled over with his sword still brandished. "Blargh... Hack, hack..." He hit the ground hard and coughed violently.

What just happened?! I thought, beyond confused. I heard someone moan behind me.

"Urgh..."

"Lia?!" I shouted. She nestled against my body as her legs gave out from under her. "What's going on?! Stay with me, Lia!"

"*Haah, haah...* I'm in pain...and I'm so...hot...," she muttered.

I put a hand to her forehead. It was searing to the touch. *Where did this fever come from? Wait, what's this crest...* There was a dark red crest on the back of her neck. *Is this a curse?!*

Curses were a mysterious power that monsters could inflict. Almost nothing was known about their effects, what triggered them, or how to dispel them.

Oh yeah, Lia said demons are a superior species of monster, so it isn't surprising that Seele can inflict curses. When did he inflict it on her, though?!

I pondered over how he could have possible done this, only to notice that the senior holy knights were collapsing one after another.

"You can't be serious..."

I looked around and saw everyone on the ground breathing raggedly. I was the only person left standing. *Did he hex everyone here at the same time?!* Rodis had a dark red crest on his right hand, the empress had one on her chest, Shii had one on the back of her neck, and everyone else had one, too. They had all been defeated in an instant, without even knowing how Seele had attacked them.

"Why did my Execration not work on you...?" the demon wondered aloud as I agonized over the dire situation. He swung his sword up at me.

"...?!" I quickly drew my blade with my left hand to block his swing backhanded.

"Wow, nice reaction speed. Your defensive skill isn't bad, either," Seele complimented.

Sparks flew from our blades. I drew Lia close and stepped back quickly to gain some distance.

I need to dispel this curse quickly...

I touched my darkness to the dark red crest on Lia's neck as she panted raggedly, and it disappeared. Her breathing stabilized as soon as it did. She was still unconscious, but her fever was gone. She would surely wake up after a little rest.

Thank goodness, I thought. *His* darkness really could do anything. It could remove any curse, whether it came from an ordinary monster or a mighty demon. *I can use this to save everyone! I just need to defeat Seele!*

I held my sword before my navel and assumed the middle posture.

"Th-that darkness... Are you a descendant of the Rodol Clan?!" Seele asked accusingly. Hatred flared in his eyes. He seemed to know something about my surname, something that clearly displeased him. "Give me your name, boy!"

It would be rude not to introduce myself after he had.

"...I'm Allen Rodol," I responded.

"I knew it! You *are* from the Rodol Clan! I didn't think finding you would be *this* easy!" Seele gave a conflicted smile and extended his right hand toward me. "I have some questions for you. Answer them with complete honesty, and I might just spare your life."

"...Are you sure you aren't confusing me for some other Rodols?" I asked.

"Ha, there's no use in playing dumb. That gloom is the symbol of the Rodol Clan. It proves your identity beyond a shadow of a doubt!" he insisted, raising his sword overhead. "If you don't want to talk, I'll just beat the answers out of you! Execration—Lightning Torture!"

Seele swung his sword down and fired pitch-black lightning from its tip. *It's fast, but not as fast as Idora!* I swung my blade at an angle to deflect the approaching lightning, but something unexpected happened.

"What the...?!" I shouted.

The pitch-black lightning wrapped around my sword like ivy, crawling down the sword and toward my body.

"Hah, taste the hellish pain of Lightning Torture!" Seele yelled, assured of his victory.

"...Huh?" I muttered in bewilderment. The ivy-like lightning turned to dust and disappeared when it touched my hand.

"Did Lightning Torture just...vanish?! Why won't curses work on you?! What's your trick?!" He pointed at me, flustered. "And more importantly, why is that darkness so wicked?! What happened to the holy darkness of the Rodol Clan?!"

"I have no idea what you're talking about..."

His darkness had been evil from the beginning. This was the first time I'd heard of a *holy* darkness.

"You're strangely immune to curses, and your darkness is nauseatingly malevolent... Are you really a member of the Rodol Clan?" Seele asked.

"Like I said, I'm a Rodol, but I'm not from this clan you keep mentioning," I responded.

I observed the room inconspicuously. *This is bad. They might not make it if this battle drags on too long.* The empress and the other people in the room were still breathing raggedly on the floor. *I wish I could go ahead and dispel everyone's curses, but Seele isn't going to give me the chance now that he's engaged me in combat. That means the best course of action is taking him out as quickly as possible!*

"Okay... Time to show you what I've got!" I declared. I gripped the mock black sword tightly and entered striking range with a single step.

"Hmph, you're charging right at me? How boring. Execration—Water Torture!" Seele snapped his fingers and a dark flash flood appeared out of nowhere. It turned to black particles and vanished when it touched my body. "Even Water Torture won't work?!"

I took advantage of Seele's momentary perturbance to strike at him with eight slashes.

"Eighth Style—Eight-Span Crow!" I shouted.

"That's too weak!" Seele yelled. He quickly drew his sword and perfectly deflected my Eight-Span Crow, sending eight sparks flying through the air. I swung my blade down at an angle in pursuit.

"*Hragh!*"

"Not good enough!"

Seele brandished his weapon with the exact same trajectory as mine. Our blades clanged violently.

"Haaaaaaaaah!"

"Oooooooooh!"

We screamed with our swords locked, each trying to overpower the other.

"You may be immune to curses, but you're still a feeble human. You have no chance against me!"

"Ngh?!"

The demon won the contest of strength, sending me flying backward. I spun in midair and landed gracefully.

He's absurdly powerful... It was no wonder he considered humans an inferior race to demons. *This is a problem.* Physical might was the foundation of all swordcraft; this fight was going to be difficult if he had the advantage in that area. *I don't want to play my hand before I know his full potential, but the empress and the others are in danger. This is the only option I have.*

I exhaled vigorously and called the name of my Soul Attire.

"Destroy—Rapacious Demon Zeon!"

The true black sword appeared through a rift in the air. The entire weapon—from blade to handle to guard—was pitch-black. I grabbed the hilt, and a surge of darkness erupted from it.

All right, this will give me a chance! Tremendous power rose from deep within me, and my five senses sharpened. I clad myself in a thick cloak of darkness.

"I-is that ebon blade what I think it is?!" Seele gasped, trembling at the sight of my Soul Attire. "I see, that's what happened... That explains why curses won't work, why the darkness is so repulsive..." He twisted his lips into a sneer. "But you have yet to mature."

"What do you mean?" I asked.

"You have yet to achieve any mastery of your abilities. The fact my head is still attached to my body is proof of that," he responded, patting his neck. "If you had total control of your power, you would have killed me at least seven times over already."

Seele seemed to know something about Zeon. And despite his arrogance, he even admitted he would stand no chance against its full potential.

"That's enough chit-chat. I'm defeating you here and now! I must do whatever it takes to remove you from the world before someone raises you into an invincible monster!" Seele yelled, tossing his sword behind him. So demons could use *that* power, too. "Beguile with Quiet Beauty—Morsa Vector!"

An ominous Soul Attire tore through the air. Seele grabbed it and pointed the tip at me.

"Allen Rodol. I'm going to kill you for the order and stability of the world!" he declared.

"You'll pay for trying to hurt Lia!" I yelled.

And so my battle with Seele Grazalio began.

■

I carefully observed Seele's Soul Attire, which he called Morsa Vector. It was a longsword, whose blade was peppered with small holes. I had never seen anything like it.

This is a demonic Soul Attire. I need to exercise extreme caution.

My opponent was a tremendously powerful demon who could use the mysterious power of Execration to defeat over a hundred senior holy knights in seconds. I could tell by the confidence he had in his Soul Attire that it was no ordinary weapon.

The best thing to do when you're unfamiliar with your opponent's ability is to attack! I needed to bear down aggressively on Seele and goad him into using his abilities to defend. I couldn't afford to let him get the first strike when I didn't yet know what he was capable of.

I reflected further on what swordcraft textbooks said about fighting an opponent with Soul Attire, then tightened my grip on Zeon. *I need to keep this quick. I'll overpower Seele with a relentless chain of attacks!*

After determining my strategy, I decided to launch a projectile slash attack to help myself get closer to him. "First Style—Flying Shadow!" The pitch-black arc raced toward Seele, tearing up the palace floor as it went.

"Hmm. You're quite strong, but that's still not good enough to harm a demon. Hah!" he said, swinging his blade sideways and easily deflecting Flying Shadow. But then he widened his eyes in astonishment. "That was a distraction?!"

After hiding behind the Flying Shadow to close the gap between us, I let my momentum carry me into my fastest move.

"Seventh Style—Draw Flash!"

My swing surpassed the speed of sound as I slashed Seele's chest.

"Hah, you missed."

The demon turned into mist before my eyes and disappeared.

"What?!" I cried, just as I heard the sound of slicing wind at my back. "You're behind me?!" I twisted around, narrowly avoiding a sharp thrust that passed before my eyes.

I instantly jumped backward to put space between us. *What just happened?!* I'd definitely just sliced Seele in the chest. I saw it clearly, and felt the move in my hands. And yet his chest was conspicuously free of a slash wound.

Did he dodge Draw Flash? No, that was impossible. There was no way he could've avoided it from that distance.

"Heh-heh, what's wrong? You look like you've seen a ghost," Seele taunted, obviously trying to provoke me.

Okay, calm down... Think about what just happened. I exhaled a large breath and thought back on that inexplicable exchange. *I absolutely slashed the Seele who was in front of me in that moment. There's no doubt about that. But then a different Seele appeared immediately after that. That shouldn't be possible, which must mean he used Morsa Vector's ability to make it happen. Was it an illusion, a clone, or something else entirely? I still don't know enough to determine what his Soul Attire is capable of.*

He must have used his Soul Attire while I'd been approaching him behind Flying Shadow. The projectile slash obstructed my vision, so I would've missed it. If he did anything, it had to have been then.

I'll charge straight at him this time, without any tricks! I would use my strike as an opportunity to closely observe Seele and figure out Morsa Vector's ability. That was how I would bring him down.

"Let's do this!" I shouted, shifting my weight down and bending forward.

"Heh-heh. Try all you want, you can't harm me!" he responded with a shrug. He looked totally nonchalant.

I took a big step forward and entered range for a deadly blow. *All right, what's he gonna do?!* I kept my eyes peeled and observed his every movement.

Seele raised his blade overhead in a peculiar trajectory and held it there with the tip pointing at me. The position left his abdomen completely unguarded. He prioritized adopting this strange stance over dodging my approaching blade or counterattacking.

Whoa, what was that?! I heard a faint sound that resembled a flute.

"Seventh Style—Draw Flash!" I shouted, successfully slicing Seele with my swift move. His form dispersed once again.

"Hah! What did I tell you?"

Seele appeared behind me again and thrust his sword three times with intent to kill.

"Grk!"

I managed to block the first two stabs, but the last pierced my left shoulder.

Oh, that's what he's doing! Everything clicked. That last exchange was enough for me to figure out Seele's ability.

"Morsa Vector's ability is sound-based, isn't it?" I asked.

"Oh? You heard the ultrasonic waves as we fought? You have sharp ears," Seele responded. He swung his Soul Attire, and it made a faint, flute-like sound as wind passed through the holes.

"Your Soul Attire plays patterns of notes and causes anyone who hears them to see illusions… Is that right?" I surmised. The two Seeles I'd just slashed were probably illusions.

"You're so close, yet so far. Morsa Vector's ability isn't so simple as that! Magic Flute—Iron Verse!"

Seele swung his blade three times with fluid, dance-like movements. A strange melody reverberated throughout the hall, and a red, blood-like substance coiled around his arms and legs.

"...Is that a physical-strengthening ability?" I asked.

"Behold my overwhelming might! My limbs are much more powerful than before! Hah!" Seele shouted, striking the floor with his Soul Attire. His blow left a large crater.

That's some incredible force. Typically, an increase in strength of that sort could only be attained with self-strengthening Soul Attire.

"I'm not done! Magic Flute—Phantom Verse!" he yelled, splitting his form into four versions of himself.

"What?!" I gasped.

"My copies may just be illusions produced by your brain, but I recommend you don't take them lightly. The shock of being sliced by an illusion will make the pain feel oh-so-real! I can take control of a person's auditory senses to fluster their brain and rewrite reality! Such is the fearsome hypnosis ability of Morsa Vector!"

The four demons adopted the exact same stance and charged simultaneously.

""""Allen Rodol! I'm going to kill you here and now, before you bring about a cataclysm!"""""

They assaulted me with downward swings, thrusts, horizontal sweeps, and more, all performed with intent to kill.

"That's definitely a formidable ability, but...is that all it can do?" I asked. I swung Zeon sideways to release a black flash of light that smothered the four demons in darkness.

""""Whuh?!"""""

The three illusions vanished, and the real Seele fell to his knees, heavily wounded.

"I-impossible... How can you manage such strength in your immature state?!" he cried, finally staring at me with fear in his eyes.

Iron Verse, which increases his strength, and Phantom Verse, which creates illusions, are both tricky abilities. But when it comes to pure power, my darkness has a massive edge. Now that I've figured out his ability, it's time to go on the offensive!

I held the black sword in the middle stance as Seele stood up, swaying like a ghost as he did so.

"I have to kill you...no matter what!" He glared at me with bloodshot eyes and gripped Morsa Vector as hard as he could.

Why was he so intent on taking my life? What was this Rodol Clan he kept mentioning? How did he know about Zeon? *I have so many questions, but there's no time to talk. I need to defeat Seele quickly and dispel everyone's curses!* I could get my answers from him after this was over.

"Take this!" I shouted, summoning even more darkness and racing toward him as fast as I could.

"S-such speed!" Seele gasped, unable to react before I reached point-blank range. He was completely defenseless.

"Cherry Blossom Blade Secret Technique—Mirror Sakura Slash!"

Four quick black slashes descended upon him from both the left and right.

"..."

Seele leaped backward, looking as though he knew wouldn't be able to dodge all eight slashes.

"Ngh..."

The projectiles cut into his arms and legs, sending blood flying.

One more push...! I thought as I bent forward in pursuit.

"Damn it... I'm a demon! There's no way you can defeat me!" Seele gave an earsplitting shout, and his injuries closed before my eyes. The chest wound from Draw Flash and the arm and leg wounds from

Mirror Sakura Slash were healed almost instantly. "How do you like that? Demonic recovery is in another league compared to how you inferior humans heal!"

"That's definitely impressive, but...why didn't you heal your wounds right after I injured you?" I asked.

Pain and blood loss slowed the body. It would only be rational to use a healing ability that impressive immediately after being wounded. He must have held off for a particular reason.

"Either you can only use it a certain number of times, or it expends a lot of stamina or spirit power. It must have some sort of limitation," I said in conjecture.

"Hah, a foolish assumption. Demons are the ultimate beings, the peak of the ecosystem. We have no such limits!" he shouted.

"Uh, if you say so... Hah!"

I dashed at him and swung my sword, kicking off a fierce sword fight. Sparks flew as our blades collided again and again.

"*Haah!*" I shouted.

"Gnnrgh..." Seele grunted.

Every deep wound I inflicted during our fight closed instantaneously. *But his recovery power is clearly slowing. Turns out he was bluffing after all. Demons clearly can't heal forever.* With every wound that healed, Seele's breathing grew more ragged, and his movements dulled. That suggested his healing ability was limited by either stamina or spirit power.

Our blades continued to collide until we ended up in another sword lock.

"Haaaaaaah!"

"Oooooooh!"

I'd lost the first time this happened because of his naturally superior demonic strength, but...

"*Hragh!*"

...I easily overpowered him with the additional might I'd gained after summoning Zeon.

"Damn it!" Seele yelled after I sent him flying. He flapped his wings quickly and regained his balance in the air. "*Haah, haah...* Magic Flute—Blade Verse!"

He waved his sword quickly, summoning hundreds of naked blades that shot toward me simultaneously. I'd always struggled with multi-hit long-distance attacks, but I had a way to deal with them now.

"Dark Shadow!" I shouted, sending forth a giant mass of darkness that swallowed the blades like a whale devouring krill.

"Damn, that's a powerful ability...," Seele said, clicking his tongue in displeasure.

"I wouldn't take your eyes off it just yet, Seele," I warned.

Dark Shadow wasn't finished—it rushed toward the demon after consuming the blades.

"What...?!" he shouted, just before the tremendously powerful gloom swallowed him whole where he hovered in the air. "Argh..."

Seele crashed hard to the floor, ragged and beaten.

"*Haah... Haah...*"

He was still breathing faintly, but his self-healing was very sluggish. He couldn't have much stamina and spirit power left.

I've won. Seele wouldn't be able to continue fighting in that state. *All right, I need to remove everyone's curses while I have the chance*, I thought, dispelling my cloak of darkness.

"This aggravates me to no end, but...I have no choice but to withdraw," Seele said, flapping his tattered wings to lift himself into the air. "Don't think that you've won, Allen Rodol. Just learning your whereabouts is a sufficient outcome. I'll come back with a hundred of my brethren next time and give you a real bloodbath! We'll slaughter every filthy human in the land!" An intense hatred shined in his eyes as he hurled his threats.

"Do you really think you can escape with those wounds of yours?" I responded.

Just a single demon had inflicted all this damage; a hundred of them would lay waste to Liengard. *I have to kill Seele before he gets away!* I focused a massive amount of spirit power into the black sword and prepared to use Dark Boom.

"Hah, the volume of your darkness continues to astonish me... But are you sure you want to do this?" Seele asked.

"What do you mean?" I responded.

"You could absolutely finish me off with that attack. But if you try, everyone else in this room will die too." He smiled viciously and swung Morsa Vector. "Magic Flute—Annihilation Verse!"

Thousands of white blades appeared and trained themselves on Lia and everyone else in the hall.

"Hey, that's messed up!" I shouted. Realizing that he couldn't defeat me one-on-one, Seele had used the last of his strength to take Lia and the others hostage.

"Heh-heh... So what'll it be? Unleash that attack, and I kill everyone here. Let me go, and I spare their lives. It's your choice," he said with an expression of ease.

I could use Dark Shadow to consume all the blades... No, that's impossible. There are too many for me to reach in time... I couldn't let Seele escape. If he came back with a hundred demons, they would turn Liengard into a literal hellscape. But...he had Lia, Shii, the empress, and all the senior holy knights by the throat. I couldn't just let them die.

"...Fine. You can go. Just don't hurt Lia and the others," I said reluctantly.

"Heh-heh-heh... Wa-ha-ha-ha! That naivete is one of your inferior race's fatal flaws!" Seele mocked, laughing triumphantly.

I then heard a voice in my head. *Listen up, brat. I'm lending you my power. Kill that demonic bastard before he can inform anyone of your whereabouts.*

It all happened in less than a second.

"...Huh?" I said.

"Impossible!" Seele gasped.

Darkness of otherworldly power engulfed the entirety of Liengard Palace, consuming the thousands of blades pointed at its occupants in an instant.

"Such absurd spirit power... So you're in there after all, Zeon!" Seele yelled, his voice rich with anger and fear. His face was pale.

...*Thanks*, I thought. I had no idea why my Spirit Core had helped me, but I would now be able to eliminate Seele without reservations. I focused spirit power into the black sword and aimed my weapon at the demon.

"No, this can't be happening... No, no, NOOOOO!"

Seele screamed and turned to flee as fast as he could. I summoned all the gloom I had, and it overflowed from the palace, spilling out on to the streets of Aurest.

"Th-that's absurd... How can he produce this much?!" the demon shouted, pausing.

His darkness was endlessly cold, endlessly black, and endlessly wicked. It was enough to make Seele gulp.

"You did this to yourself," I said.

"..."

He had attacked Lia and the others twice. I couldn't let him get away with that.

"You're done, Seele!" I lifted the ebon blade overhead, and my darkness blanketed the sky.

"NOOOOOOOO!"

Seele shook free from his stupor and flapped his wings desperately, flying away from Liengard Palace. I took careful aim and put all my strength into my attack.

"Sixth Style—Dark Boom!" I yelled, sending a slash thick enough to cast a shadow racing toward him with incredible speed.

"DAMN YOU, FILTHY HUMAAAAAN!" he yelled as Dark Boom hit him directly, coating him in darkness and sending him tumbling into a forest outside of Aurest.

Man, he's strong. Seele was still moving slightly after getting hit. *Demons really are something else...* He had a tough body, incredible recovery ability, and astounding stamina; his physical ability far surpassed that of humanity. *I hurt him badly, though. He's not going anywhere for a while. My top priority is dispelling everyone's curses.*

I moved to heal everyone and heard *his* displeased voice in my mind again.

What're you doing, you damn brat?! Go snuff him out, now! He may be a wimp, but demons are way harder to kill than humans. He'll escape while you're loafin' around here!

"Just hang on a minute. I'll go after Seele after I dispel everyone's curses," I responded.

Some of the senior holy knights were beginning to spasm from the pain of their hexes. They could die if I left them alone any longer.

Who cares about these dregs?! Don't you realize what's at stake?! You're gonna be in deep shit if you let that demon get away! he seethed.

"I know that. But even so...I can worry about myself later. I'm going to heal everyone first."

It wouldn't take more than two or three minutes to heal everyone here. I could spare that amount of time.

Geez, your stubbornness and naïvete remind me a lot of them...

"'Them'? Who are you talking about?" I asked.

No one. Forget about that, he answered, unusually inarticulate. *Anyway, don't you dare let that demon escape. Got it?*

"Yeah, I know."

We could kiss Liengard goodbye if Seele got away. I couldn't allow that to happen.

Not wanting to waste any more time, I used my darkness to remove all the scarlet crests on everyone's bodies, dispelling Seele's curses.

"Phew... That's that," I said after removing everyone's curses. I could finally take a breather.

They're all still asleep, though... Not a single person had woken up. The hex must have taken more out of them than I realized. *I did heal them, right...?* I thought, feeling a bit anxious.

"Nnn..."

I looked down and saw Lia slowly waking up. She was the first one I'd healed; my treatment must've worked.

"Lia! Thank goodness! Do you feel okay?!" I asked.

"Huh? What do you... Oh yeah, where's the demon?!" she responded, jumping to her feet and drawing her sword. She looked perfectly healthy.

"Don't worry. I already defeated him."

"What?! You defeated him all by yourself?!"

"Yeah. It was pretty tough, though."

"I really shouldn't let anything you do surprise me at this point...," Lia said, sounding a little exasperated. She inspected the hall. "Where is he? Did you...totally wipe him out?"

"No, I didn't go that far. He tried to fly away, so I knocked him out of the sky with a Dark Boom," I answered.

"Wow, you beat that arrogant demon so bad he had to cut and run..."

"Anyway, Seele is in a nearby forest. I want to go catch him as quickly as possible. Would you mind protecting everyone here while I'm gone?"

I couldn't leave everyone unguarded while they were unconscious.

"No, not at all. But be careful. You don't know what that demon is capable of. Come back if things get too dangerous, okay?" Lia urged.

"Got it," I responded.

I left Liengard Palace to go to the nearby forest and capture Seele.

■

In a forest located just outside of Aurest, Seele Grazalio crawled across the ground, covered in grievous wounds.

"Haah, haah..."

His failed attempt to erase Allen Rodol had him feeling more humiliated than he had in his entire life.

Damn it all to hell... How did this happen?

Hatred welled inside him, fueled by his fury at the ragged state of his body. His healing ability was still working sluggishly.

You will pay for this, Allen Rodol!

He fought to drag himself along, willed by his hatred of his new sworn enemy.

I have to return and tell my brethren what I've learned about him...

Seele continued to crawl, desperate to escape Allen Rodol.

"Oh? Found him, Rize! I think this is the demon we're looking for!"

Just then, a suspicious-looking man in a clown outfit emerged from the trees. It was Clown Jester.

"Let me see... Oh dear, Allen didnae hold back with him."

A woman with fox-like eyes wearing an elegant kimono appeared next. It was Rize Dorhein.

"...Oh, it's just some inferiors," Seele said after noticing the unfamiliar humans. He sighed with relief. He could immediately kill any human with a curse as long as they weren't an exception like Allen. "I don't have time to deal with scum like you two. Execration—Fire Torture."

An invisible curse swept toward the two humans...

"Desiccate—Withered Parasol."

...But then it disappeared due to some unknown power.

"My, no need tae be so violent. Would ye care tae have a wee chat?" Rize said, cackling.

"Wh-why didn't my curse work... Don't tell me you—," Seele's voice cut off and he grabbed his throat. *Wh-why can't I breathe?! How is this filthy human...doing this...?*

Seele passed out from severe oxygen deficiency.

"We've captured the target. Clown, take him tae my mansion before Allen gets here," Rize commanded.

"You got it! Oh man... I've always wanted a demon body to play around with!" Clown said, picking Seele up with an insane smile. The demon disappeared from his arms immediately afterward. "Huh?"

"Hyo-hoh-hoh. My apologies, but I'll be taking custody of that creature."

Rize and Clown turned around to see a short old man. His hair and beard were snow-white, his back was bent, and he held a cane in one hand. Seele was at his feet, bound with rope.

What the heck? How did he take Seele from me? Clown thought. It was inexplicable. When had the old man approached him, grabbed the demon, and walked away? Clown was an elite swordsman, but he hadn't sensed him at all. It was as if the old man had stopped time itself. *It could've been a Soul Attire ability...*

"Well, well... This is quite the honor. I've always wanted tae meet ye, Time Hermit," Rize said.

"Hyo-hoh? To think I'd hear that from such a beautiful lady at this age... Growing old isn't so bad after all," the Time Hermit muttered happily.

"What dae ye want with this demon?" Rize asked.

"Hyo-hoh-hoh. I couldn't care less about this creature. But if you insist on hearing a reason for my actions... I'm just trying to restrict certain information from getting out."

"Huh... First Zeon, and now the Time Hermit. What are ye two plotting?"

"You know about *him*? Now, that's a surprise... You two are treading a dangerous path for ones so young." The Time Hermit nodded repeatedly as if impressed. His expression then turned serious. "I am acting on a pledge I made long ago. Young folk such as yourselves should not get involved."

He clearly wasn't going to reveal anything else.

Seconds later, about ten meters of ground around the old man caved in. The unknown power crushed trees in the area, pulverized rocks, and tore up the earth. It was an immense display of destruction.

"Hyo-hoh-hoh! You're quite powerful!"

The Time Hermit laughed gleefully after easily dodging Clown's invisible assault. Seele remained at the old man's feet, also untouched by the attack.

"Guess that's your 'transparency' ability I've heard about. Sure looks useful…," Clown said, his curiosity piqued.

"Stop," Rize commanded, seeing that the Time Hermit was about to unleash an even stronger attack. "We don't have time fae a grueling fight with him. Allen will be here any second. Let's withdraw."

"…Fine. *Haah*, It's such a shame to lose such a valuable test subject…," Clown responded dejectedly, shoulders drooping. He cut off his spirit power.

"Hey, Time Hermit. How would ye like to tae meet for tea next time?" Rize asked.

"Hyo-hoh! I couldn't possibly refuse an invitation from a woman of your beauty! Give me the time and place, and I'll be there!" the Time Hermit exclaimed.

"Hee-hee, ye're quite the flatterer. Until next time."

Rize and Clown walked away into the trees.

"Hmm, it was definitely the right call to show my face…," the Time Hermit muttered, looking down at the unconscious demon he'd captured. He left a message in ancient script that only Zeon would be able to read. "I suppose I'll get back to fishing…"

The old man disappeared into the depths of the forest, dragging Seele behind him.

■

After dispelling everyone's curses, I ran toward the woods to capture Seele.

It's crazy out here… Mass hysteria gripped Aurest as I raced through the streets. Some people were sprinting to get as far from Liengard

Palace as they could, others were hurrying to close their shops, and many were petrified in place, unsure of what to do.

I reached the forest Seele had crashed into and quickly waded through the thick vegetation. *I'm sure he landed around here*, I thought once I reached the area where it looked like he'd fallen after I hit him with Dark Boom. *He's too injured to have gone far. Demons recover incredibly quickly, though. It's been about ten minutes since I knocked him out of the sky. I can't waste any more time. He'll be able to fly away if his wings recover.*

I moved deeper into the woods while keeping my eyes peeled for any sign of Seele, and found an unbelievable sight.

"What happened here?!"

Something had devastated a small section of the forest, leaving the ground cratered, trees smashed, and rocks crumbled. It was almost as if gravity had been increased by a hundredfold in this spot alone, destroying everything in range to form a clearing.

"Did Seele do this?"

I traced a finger along the crater in the ground as I wondered how this happened. *It's damp. That means the damage is recent. Was it Seele who did this, or some other threat entirely? Whoever it was, they're clearly very powerful.*

I quietly drew my sword and looked around. Then *he* spoke in my mind.

Hey, brat.

"What is it?" I asked.

There's something written under that tree.

"I'm going to need you to be a bit more specific..."

I wasn't sure which tree he meant, but I looked around and eventually found something at the foot of a large tree.

"What's this?" I said. There were strange lines drawn there. "Are these...characters?" The lines had an orderly nature to them, but I had never seen writing like it before. Was it a demon language, or some kind of code?

So that's what happened... Hey, we're good here.

"Huh? What do you mean?"

We don't gotta worry about that demon anymore. I'm going to sleep.

I pressed my Spirit Core for an explanation multiple times, but he didn't respond.

"Geez, he's so difficult..."

Well, he sounded pretty sure about it. It was probably fine. *I wish he would tell me why we don't have to worry about the demon, but...I know him. He's never that nice to me.*

"Haah... Guess I'll just go back..."

Having done a whole bunch of nothing, I turned around to return to Liengard Palace.

◼

Still feeling unsatisfied, I retraced the path I'd taken to the forest and went back to Liengard Palace, which was now just a single story tall.

Man, the palace is in terrible shape... The residence of the empress now looked like a ruin. *One demon did all this.*

I thought back to the battle. Seele was a fearsome opponent. He could inflict curses with his strong Execration ability, his strength far surpassed that of humans, he recovered from injury astoundingly quickly, and worst of all, he didn't hesitate to kill. Human lives meant nothing to him because he saw us as inferior.

Barel Ronelia said that the Holy Ronelian Empire brokered a pact of friendship with five demons... That meant they were in league with four more demons who were likely as strong as Seele, if not more powerful. Just thinking about it gave me a headache.

I wonder what the fallout of this is going to be...? The assault on the palace was clearly an act of war, one in which the Holy Ronelian Empire had delivered the first blow against Liengard. *I don't know how the empress will respond, but it's easy to see a violent collision with the Holy Empire on the horizon.*

If worse came to worst, this could start a world war.

I feel depressed..., I thought, stepping into the palace.

Lia spotted me right away. "Allen! I'm so glad you're okay!" she said, running toward me happily.

"Thanks... Looks like everyone here is doing all right," I responded. The empress and the others were on their feet and in seemingly good health.

"They're all feeling great, thanks to you."

"That's good to hear."

The empress approached us as we spoke.

"Thank you so much for all you've done today, Mr. Rodol. You deserve a medal for the incredible feats of fighting off the demon and dispelling the curses he inflicted. I thank you on behalf of the people of Liengard," she said, sounding every part the empress. It was amazing how well she could hide her true nature.

"There's no need to thank me. I just did what was right," I responded.

The empress leaned forward and whispered in my ear. "I just *love* that modest and straightforward personality of yours... I hope we can have some more fun together, Allen."

"Ah-ha-ha... Try to control yourself next time."

"Hmm-hmm, I'll think about it."

The empress walked back toward the senior holy knights.

Looks like I've caught the attention of another pain of a person..., I thought, sighing internally. Someone patted me on the shoulder, and I turned around to find Rodis Arkstoria.

"...Allen Rodol. It seems you have stronger moral fiber than the rumors would have one believe," he said before staring at me.

"M-Mr. Rodis...?" I stammered.

"I may eventually come to accept you...if you start as friends."

"Huh?"

"Hmph. Must I spell it out? I'm talking about your relationship with Shii."

"Oh, okay..."

The demon attack had totally driven our last conversation from my mind.

"It is thanks to your heroics that Liengard avoided ruin. I will tolerate your presence around my daughter as long as you remain one unremarkable friend among her countless existing companions," Rodis said.

"Ah-ha-ha... I'm honored," I responded.

It took saving the country for him to approve of me as Shii's friend. *What would I have to do to get him to let me date her? Conquer the world?* I thought, smiling awkwardly.

Then I noticed a suspicious group of people huddled in the corner of the hall. They were glancing at me repeatedly and whispering to each other.

"Wh-what should we do?! This could be a rare chance to tie ourselves to Allen Rodol!"

"The stories about him are concerning, but his strength is the real deal. It could be a boon to network with him..."

"Wouldn't that be dangerous? They say he's close with the Blood Fox..."

"I don't care who he's associated with! I'm talking to him! We just saw that he's powerful enough to fight off a demon all on his own! Having a relationship with him could only be a good thing!"

"W-wait! I'm not letting you get the jump on us!"

The people raised their voices until they started shouting at each other, before they abruptly stopped and ran over to me with determination.

"Greetings, Lord Allen! You really distinguished yourself today! I would love to introduce myself—"

"Lord Allen! Ignore that worthless moneylender and come with me—"

"Don't listen to him! I'm the manager of Garbest Real Estate, a company of some renown in Aurest! A connection with me could benefit you in the—"

"No, Allen—"

"Please, Allen—"

They all held out their business cards, getting more and more riled up until they began to fight with each other.

"Uhh...," I said, unsure of what was happening.

Lia dragged me away by the sleeve. "Let's go before we get roped into anything else, Allen," she urged.

"Good idea," I responded. I politely refused the suspicious people and returned to Thousand Blade with Lia.

The New Year's Jubilee had been more turbulent than I could've imagined, but somehow, someway, we'd survived it.

CHAPTER 3
The Allen Cell & a Political Marriage

It was the second day of the new year. I was enjoying a quiet, peaceful morning, which was much needed after the chaos of the New Year's Jubilee.

I glanced at the clock. It was seven in the morning, a perfect time to wake up.

"Ngh…"

I got out of bed and stretched widely.

"Good morning, Allen," Lia said, showing herself from the kitchen. She had already gotten herself ready for the day. She looked lovely in her white apron.

"*Hraah…* G'morning, Lia," I responded.

"Hmm-hmm, feeling groggy?"

"Yeah, a little."

I'd drained a lot of spirit power using all that darkness yesterday. My body still felt sluggish.

"Do you want me to make breakfast a little later than usual?" she asked, holding a frying pan.

"No, you can make it at the usual time. I don't want to throw off my day," I responded.

"Okay. It'll be ready in a bit."

"Thanks so much."

I washed my face, brushed my teeth, and put on my uniform as she prepared breakfast. It was winter break, so I could have just worn my personal clothes, but Thousand Blade students were encouraged to wear their uniforms when going out. Besides, they were also made to handle intense combat, so they were elastic, stab-proof, and durable. The world was growing increasingly dangerous, and I never knew when I could get roped into a fight. I always wore my uniform for that reason, unless special circumstances demanded otherwise.

I'm ready to go, I thought.

Lia called out just when I finished getting dressed. "Allen, breakfast is ready!"

"Coming!"

◼

Lia's breakfast was a well-balanced, nutritional meal consisting of miso soup, broiled fish, boiled spinach, and white rice.

"Wow, this looks delicious!" I said.

"Hmm-hmm, let's eat while it's warm," Lia replied.

We sat in chairs across from each other and put our hands together.

""Thank you for the food.""

I reached for the miso soup first.

"Ahh… It's so nice and warm," I said.

The soup stock was healthy and only moderately salted, the tofu was cut into small cubes, and the wakame was a great complement. It was the perfect dish for a cold winter morning.

After being warmed by the soup, I moved on to the fish and spinach. Lia's cooking was delicious, as per usual.

"Do you like it?" Lia asked with a smile.

"Yeah, it's amazing," I replied.

"Hee-hee, I'm glad to hear it."

We continued to eat, sharing another happy breakfast.

Chapter 3

"*"That hit the spot!"*"

We carried our dishes to the sink after we finished eating. It was my job to wash them after a meal. Lia always said that she would do it, but I would've felt guilty if I didn't at least help her out after she cooked such delicious food for me.

Lia chatted with me as I scrubbed hard at the dishes. "Oh yeah, they wrote about yesterday's incident in the paper."

"Really? What does it say?" I asked.

"Let's see... *Demon attack at Liengard Palace! The Empress is unhurt due to the heroics of a local swordsman!* That's the headline."

"That's not very specific..."

"The government probably restricted the information they could print. There's no mention of Seele's name, the curses, or you," she said as she flipped through the newspaper.

"I see... I don't really get why they'd do that, but whatever. I just want to enjoy a relaxing New Year's today," I replied.

Yesterday started with the New Year's Jubilee and ended with a demon attack. It was a chaotic start to the year, and I wanted to wash my hands of it. *I have a feeling this year is going to be even crazier than the last...* I sighed internally.

"Oh yeah. Do you want to go visit a shrine for the new year, Allen?" Lia asked.

"Hmm... Do you have somewhere in mind?" I responded.

"...! I do, actually! This is just an idea, but—," she began excitedly, but was interrupted when someone knocked on our door.

"Who would visit us this early in the morning?" I wondered.

"It could be Rose or Claude... Or Reia, maybe?" Lia said.

Rose was bad with mornings, so she seemed like an unlikely candidate. Claude had been staying far away from our dorm. It seemed like she was trying to be considerate, but it made me feel a little awkward.

That left Chairwoman Reia. *Wait a second... Where is she? Now that I think about it, I didn't see her at the New Year's Jubilee. It's unlike her to not show up at such a major incident. Maybe work has taken her out of Aurest?*

"Well, I'm gonna see who it is," I said.

"Okay. Be careful," Lia responded.

"Will do."

I grabbed my sword just in case and went to the door.

"Who is it?" I asked as I slowly opened the door. I was greeted by the sight of over one hundred holy knights, all kneeling before me. "U-uhh...?"

I stood there baffled until one of them spoke up.

"Greetings, Mr. Rodol. Could you please come to Liengard Palace with us? Her Majesty awaits," he said.

Welp, so much for my day of relaxation. *The empress is summoning me, huh...* I wasn't too excited to see her considering it was only a day after she assaulted me, but she was the ruler of Liengard. Refusal wasn't an option.

I have to go, don't I...? I thought with a small sigh.

"Is everything okay, Allen...? What the heck?!" Lia peeked out the door and reacted with shock upon seeing over one hundred holy knights kneeling to me.

"They said the empress has summoned me for some reason," I explained.

"H-huh. It looks like she sent a whole army to escort you..."

"No kidding..."

There was no way any sensible person could justify sending one hundred holy knights to escort an ordinary person like me. As someone who'd grown up poor, the waste of personnel made me feel really uncomfortable.

How long are they going to stay down like that? The holy knights' presence was stifling as they continued to kneel in silence.

"Umm... Can you all please act normally?" I asked.

There was a cluster of Thousand Blade dorms in this area, which was a fact that I greatly resented at this moment; the stares of the students leaving them to train or visit a shrine made me want to melt into the floor. But the worst part was that no one seemed to question the giant crowd of kneeling holy knights as soon as they saw at me. They all gave me an expression that said, *Oh, that makes sense*, and quickly walked away.

This was almost certainly going to give people another terrible misunderstanding. *I don't think my reputation could possibly get any worse... But there has to be something I can do. Catching anything that could lead to a misunderstanding and nipping it in the bud should help eradicate the bad rumors over time... At least, I hope so.*

The holy knight kneeling in front spoke, snapping me back to reality. "My apologies, but Her Majesty said to treat you as a state guest. I ask for your understanding."

"Did she...?" I responded. I supposed this was what being treated as a state guest entailed.

"Please come with us to Liengard Palace, Mr. Rodol!"

""""Please, Mr. Rodol!""""

A loud chorus of deep voices reverberated throughout Thousand Blade as they pleaded with me to accompany them to the palace. That brought even more stares my way.

"Man, it's the second day of the year and Allen's already bagged himself an army of senior holy knights... That guy has no chill."

"They say he's conspiring with a demon. He let it attack Liengard Palace so he could make a deal with the empress..."

"Geez, are you serious? I've heard he's connected to the Blood Fox, too. I'd believe anything about that guy at this point..."

I had been through this enough times to know that bad rumors were being born that very moment. They would deliver yet another blow to my reputation. Just great.

"O-okay, okay! I'll go with you to see Her Majesty! Can you please raise your heads?!"

"Wonderful! Thank you, Mr. Rodol!" the holy knight at the front exclaimed.

""""Thank you Mr. Rodol!"""" the other knights yelled together.

I hurried to my room to get ready to see the empress.

■

I left for Liengard Palace ten minutes later. Thankfully, Lia volunteered to go with me. *I'm relieved that she's coming.* The empress was significantly less likely to attack me again with a Vesterian princess present. She couldn't do something so brazen.

What in the world does she want to talk about, though? It had to have been an urgent matter if she decided to send one hundred holy knights to fetch me this early in the morning.

I continued to speculate on her motivations as we walked through the winding streets of Aurest. When we reached the palace, I was amazed to see that the first and second floors had been almost completely restored.

"Wh-what the heck?!" I said.

"This place was a ruin yesterday! How in the world is it already almost rebuilt?!" Lia exclaimed.

A holy knight explained as we stared at it in shock. "Her Majesty hired the most technologically advanced construction company in Liengard. All of their employees are skilled Soul Attire users, so they can build durably and precisely in a very short amount of time. They are scheduled to finish repairs around six in the evening."

"That's crazy," I responded. I looked around and saw brawny carpenters wielding Soul Attires on the third floor. *Man, they're all jacked.* The men had thick back muscles, developed pecs, tight quadriceps—it was clear from a distance how strong they were.

"Please enter, Mr. Rodol and Princess Lia. Her Majesty is waiting for you," a holy knight said.

We stepped inside the palace, and the holy knights guided us to a guest room on the second floor. It was another room furnished with the bare necessities. It felt less like a guest room and more like a hastily made office.

"Greetings, Mr. Rodol and Princess Lia. Thank you for coming," the empress said upon our arrival. She shoved a thick stack of papers in a drawer and moved to a four-person table in the middle of the room. "Please, be seated."

She sat in a plain wooden chair. Two brawny swordsmen stationed themselves behind her.

I think they're just guards, but they look like they want to kill me... Both men were standing on the tips of their toes, and hatred shined in their eyes. They looked ready to strike at the slightest provocation. That was definitely not normal guard behavior.

Did I do something to offend them? I wondered.

"Stand down, Gonso and Evans. That is no way to behave toward a guest that I invited," the empress chided.

"M-my apologies, Your Majesty..."

"...Sorry. I let myself get too tense."

The guards—Gonso and Evans—both apologized, but they continued to stare at me.

"*Haah...* I'm sorry about them, Mr. Rodol. They're still on edge about our little incident yesterday," the empress apologized.

"Huh...? Oh, I see," I responded. She was referring to how she'd attacked me yesterday. I looked at Gonso and Evans again and realized they were two of the guards who *he* stabbed with his darkness.

From their point of view, the empress is holding a meeting with someone who stabbed them... That would make anyone feel uneasy. I understood why they were being so wary of me.

"What's she talking about, Allen?" Lia asked, confused. She didn't know about what happened between me and the empress yesterday.

"Oh, uh... It was nothing, really. You don't have to worry about it," I answered.

"Really? If you say so..."

Not wanting to discuss the topic any further, I motioned Lia to follow me toward the table. ""Excuse us,"" we said as we sat down together.

"Mr. Rodol. I appreciate you coming all this way despite the sudden summons. Thank you for coming as well, Princess Lia," the empress said politely. "I would have liked to receive you in a proper audience chamber rather than this small room, but the palace has not yet been fully restored after yesterday's attack. I hope you can forgive me."

"Oh, it's okay. I feel more at ease in rooms like this," I replied.

"Hmm-hmm, I am relieved to hear that." Once we had gotten our greetings out of the way, the empress cleared her throat. "I summoned you here because there is a matter of utmost urgency I wish to discuss with you. It concerns the demon attack that occurred yesterday. First, I'll fill you in on the current international situation."

The empress tapped the desk, and Gonso and Evans spread a map of the world on it.

"You probably could have predicted this from Barel Ronelia's message yesterday, but a demon was dispatched to each of the Five Powers simultaneously," she said.

The Five Powers was a nickname for a group of five countries that consisted of the Liengard Empire, Lia's Vesteria Kingdom, the Commonwealth of Polyesta, the Republic of Ronzo, and the Principality of Theresia. The countries were formal allies united in opposition against the nefarious superpower that was the Holy Ronelian Empire. Needless to say, the fact that Ronelia was striking all five nations at once was world-shaking in its consequences.

This really could end up leading to a world war... The thought depressed me. And then the Empress said something that deflated my mood even more.

"The Holy Ronelian Empire conquered Theresia last night," she said.

""What?!"" Lia and I gasped.

One of the Five Powers had already been subjugated. That was a much bigger crisis than when the same happened to the small country of Daglio, the Land of Sunshine.

"It seems like Barel Ronelia launched this five-prong attack with the aim of capturing Theresia all along. According to our reports, the demon in Theresia was accompanied by three Oracle Knights and Dodriel Barton, who is known for his shadow abilities," the empress continued.

"*Three* of the Oracle Knights?!" I repeated.

Barel Ronelia had sent a tremendously powerful demon, three swordsmen with the strength of a national army, and Dodriel, whose shadow abilities made him a fearsome opponent. Their combined might was too much for Theresia to handle, since it had the weakest military of the Five Powers.

"The reports also say that Dodriel was inducted into the Thirteen Oracle Knights due to his service in this assault, filling the spot left open by Raine Grad," the empress said.

"Huh...," I responded, shocked. I didn't even know what to say to that.

"What about Vesteria?!" Lia cried, pale-faced. She must have been worried sick about her father, King Gris Vesteria. She'd lost her mother at a young age, so he was her only living relative.

"Worry not, Princess Lia. Vesteria got lucky and escaped this incident intact," the empress informed her.

"Thank goodness... But what do you mean by 'lucky'?" Lia asked, bothered by her wording.

"The demon who attacked Vesteria lacked the belligerent personality of much of its kind. According to reports, they managed to avoid combat after holding a conversation with it."

It seemed that not all demons were like Seele, who saw humans as inferior and attacked them on sight. The one who'd been sent to Vesteria sounded downright reasonable.

"I see." Lia sighed with relief.

"That's great, Lia," I said.

"Yeah. Thanks, Allen."

Now that we knew what had happened in Vesteria, I decided to ask about the other countries. "What about Polyesta and Ronzo?"

"They are fine for the time being. Polyesta and Ronzo suffered great harm, but the Seven Holy Blades were able to hasten over to both nations before they fell to the demons," the empress answered.

"Man, the Seven Holy Blades live up to their reputation," I said.

The Seven Holy Blades were employed by the Holy Knights Association and were said to be humanity's seven strongest swordfighters. They all possessed superhuman strength, polished swordcraft, and powerful Soul Attires specialized for combat. Many considered them humanity's only hope against the Ronelian Empire.

"There was very little damage here in Liengard thanks to you, Mr. Rodol… But Polyesta and Ronzo were devastated," the empress said with downcast eyes. "The demons used a terrible power called Execration to curse a great many people. This has placed the two nations—no, all of humanity—in an unprecedented crisis."

She paused briefly and looked into my eyes.

"On that point, Mr. Rodol, I have a request to make of you."

"A request…?"

"Yes. Please let us investigate that darkness of yours that can repel even curses."

"Do you mean this?"

I summoned a bit of gloom in my right palm.

"Yes, exactly. I want to learn everything we can about that ability of yours."

The empress continued talking as she stared at my darkness with great curiosity.

"Many organizations throughout the world study curses, and they've invested enormous amounts of money and brilliant research into these efforts. Yet their investigations have borne little to no fruit. We know almost nothing about how curses work or how to dispel them. But your darkness cured our hexes within seconds flat! It almost feels like we're being mocked! You have accomplished the first known instance of anyone dispelling a curse from a demon or monster, a spectacular achievement that will undoubtedly go down in history!"

The empress spoke passionately, her expression full of hope.

"And according to Rodis's report, you are completely immune to hexes as the wielder of the darkness," she said.

"I am?" I responded. Now that she mentioned it, it was possible I had some kind of resistance to curses. Seele's Fire Torture, Lightning Torture, and Water Torture hadn't worked at all on me.

"Both Polyesta and Ronzo are suffering from a terrible outbreak of curses as a result of the demon attacks. According to my sources, there are a little over one hundred thousand total victims."

"O-one hundred thousand?!"

"That's right. The doctors are only giving them a few days to live…"

"That's terrible…"

The situation was so awful that I was at a loss for words.

"Please, Mr. Rodol. Would you let us study your darkness so we can find a cure for curses?" the empress pleaded.

"Yes, of course. I'll do whatever you need of me to help all those people," I responded. Nothing would make me happier than my abilities being able to save so many lives. I wanted them to study my darkness as closely as possible to find a cure.

"Thank you very much! I knew I could count on you, Mr. Rodol!" the empress exclaimed, grabbing my hands. Her eyes were shining.

Lia's face twisted in anger.

"A-anyway, Your Majesty! How are you going to study my powers?" I asked, hurrying the conversation along.

"We are going to start by having you heal people who are suffering from curses and analyzing the process with state-of-the-art equipment. We want to discover how exactly your darkness affects curses," the empress explained.

"That makes sense."

"The research will be conducted at the Liengardian National Research Institute. It has all the latest equipment, so it's the ideal place for conducting immersive research. I've asked the world's best doctor of medicine to lead the project."

"Really? The best doctor in the entire world?"

"Yes. She's a brilliant woman who has found cures for many terrible diseases despite her young age. She's also a distinguished scientist, mathematician, and military strategist—truly one of the great minds of our time."

"Th-that's amazing..."

It sounded like a genius among geniuses would be leading the research efforts.

"She's a bit of a difficult person—no, a *very* difficult person—but her skill is the genuine article," the empress said, scratching her cheek awkwardly.

"I'll try my best not to offend her...," I replied.

This could have been my bias speaking, but I felt like most geniuses were a little off in the head. *I need to be careful with what I say around her. I don't want to get on her bad side.*

"She should be arriving any minute now..." The empress glanced at her watch just before someone knocked on the door. "Speak of the devil! That must be her. Come in!"

Chapter 3

"Greetings, Your Majesty...!" said a small girl with a meek expression as she entered the room.

She couldn't have been more than 140 centimeters tall. Her skin was so smooth and her face so childish that she didn't look old enough to buy alcohol. Her frizzy black hair reached her back. She wore a white coat many sizes too big for her, and a small sword that resembled a *wakizashi* rested at her hip.

No way!

There was no doubt about it. This was Kemmi Fasta, the chairwoman of White Lily Girls Academy.

"Hold on. This 'greatest doctor in the world' you were talking about is Chairwoman Kemmi?!" I exclaimed.

"Yes, that's correct. She serves as the chairwoman for White Lily Girls Academy in addition to all her other work. Remarkable, isn't she?" the empress responded.

"H-huh..."

That reminded me—Idora *had* called Kemmi a genius scientist during the Skills Challenge...

"Y-Your Majesty! You meant what you said, didn't you?! Tell me that wasn't a lie!" Kemmi hounded the empress, her expression tense.

"Yes, of course I did. I will give you a cash reward of one hundred million guld upon the creation of a cure for curses," the empress responded.

Kemmi had been lured onto the project at the prospect of a hefty cash prize... That was definitely on-brand for her.

"Mwa-ha-ha... That's enough money to pay off my debt and live the gambler's dream!" Kemmi laughed greedily. "All right, Allen. Time is money, as they say! Let's go bang out this hex cure! I want to get this done before I have to repay my debt in three days!"

She dashed out of the room and flew down the stairs.

"*Haah*... Well, wanna get going?" I asked Lia.

"Yeah, I guess so...," she responded.

"Mr. Rodol, Princess Lia, Chairwoman Fasta. I'm counting on you three," the empress said.

She saw me and Lia off as we left for the Liengardian National Research Institute.

■

We walked five minutes from the palace to the northeast and arrived at a large white building.

"Here we are. This is the Liengardian National Research Institute!" Kemmi announced. She inserted a card key into a machine set before the gate. The machine beeped, and the double swing gate opened slowly.

"This place is so modern...," I marveled.

"How cool is that! This feels like a secret base!" Lia exclaimed.

"Ha-ha, get used to that feeling! This is Liengard's leading research institute, after all!" Kemmi said proudly.

She walked briskly into the white, cube-like building that was the Liengardian National Research Institute. We followed her, and she guided us to the second floor.

This is wild...

An endless stream of people in white coats dashed busily about the corridors. No small number of them had dark bags under their eyes, broken glasses, or unkempt hair, and some were even muttering to themselves.

These people live in a totally different world. I couldn't see there being much overlap between the lives of swordfighters and researchers.

I continued to marvel at the unusual atmosphere of the place until Kemmi stopped in front of a room.

"This is Laboratory 3. We're going to perform the curse research in here," she announced before punching a code into an LCD screen in the middle of the door. The thick door opened on its own, and the lights turned on automatically. "After you."

"Excuse me," I said.

"Thanks," Lia responded.

Laboratory 3 was about the size of a Thousand Blade classroom and had quite an oppressive atmosphere. An examination table resembling a blue bed was set in the middle of the room and surrounded by a number of imposing machines. The devices were all unfamiliar to me, so the place felt unlike any other I'd been to.

"Okay, let's get set up!" Kemmi said. She rolled up the sleeves of her overly large coat and approached a machine. "I'll start with a simple explanation of how this research is going to go." She cleared her throat as she operated the machine with practiced hands. "A long succession of curse victims is going to be carried into this room. Please heal them all, Allen. I'm going to observe and analyze the process the darkness uses to dispel the curses."

"Understood."

My job was plain and simple—all I had to do was dispel the hexes of the patients who were carried into this room. Simple, mindless tasks were my specialty.

"Umm... Is there anything I can help with?" Lia asked, looking unsure of what to do with herself.

"Hmm... You can stand by Allen's side and support him," Kemmi said.

"Huh? Support him?"

"Yes. This research is going to be a long and grueling process. Allen will have to use his darkness the entire time without a break, which will require a massive amount of spirit power. This will exhaust him. I want you to be there for him to lessen his mental burden."

It was an established theory that one's mental state had a strong effect on their spirit power. Being weak-willed or carrying a lot of stress was said to prevent one from using their Soul Attire to its full potential.

"I can do that! Don't worry, Allen. I'll be here for you," Lia assured me.

"Thanks, that means a lot," I said.

"But, uh... How exactly do I support you?"

"Ah-ha-ha, good question."

Lia didn't have to do anything beyond standing by my side. Her simple presence would be enough to keep me at ease.

"By the way, Chairwoman Kemmi. Exactly how long will this take? The empress said the people in Polyesta and Ronzo only have a few days to live," I asked.

There were over one hundred thousand curse victims between the two nations. It was a tall order, but I wanted to find a cure within the next few days to save everyone.

"Trust me, this'll be over before then. I said it would be a long and grueling process, but if I don't find a cure in three days, my home will be seized! And I'm *not* about to let that happen..." Kemmi was facing an urgent crisis of her own. "I'm more concerned about how your body will hold up... You're going to have to use your spirit power endlessly for a few days on end. This is going to require superhuman endurance."

"I know it'll be difficult, but I can do it. I'm pretty confident in my stamina," I responded. Confident enough to know I could endure swinging my sword nonstop for over a billion years straight.

"Hah, that's exactly what I want to hear. Now, then... Time is short, so let's get started!" Kemmi said.

""Got it!""

Thus we embarked on a journey to accomplish what no person had done before—discover a cure for curses.

■

Once her machine was ready, Kemmi grabbed a microphone and spoke.

"It's time to start the Curse Cure Research Project. Please bring in the first patient," she said.

Two holy knights opened the door and walked in carrying a patient on a stretcher. They set the patient on the examination table.

"This is Gwin Arnold, sixty-five years old. He is suffering from the Erosion Curse, which slowly steals the use of one's limbs. He takes a strong painkiller every day to combat burning pain throughout his entire body. But the effects of the drugs are waning, putting him in critical condition," one of them explained.

"He was hexed in the summer of his thirty-fifth year. He was afflicted via a monster bite while working as a witchblade. The dark red crest spread from his right arm to his entire body, and thirty years later, he can't lift his head without assistance," the other continued.

One of the holy knights produced a thick stack of papers and handed it to Kemmi.

"More detailed information can be found in these documents. They are yours to reference if needed."

"Much appreciated," Kemmi said, reading the documents with astounding speed. "So we're starting with the Erosion Curse... That's setting the bar really high..."

She looked at Gwin and the documents with a difficult expression. This must have been a serious curse.

"All right, Allen. I'm ready on my end, so please begin your treatment," Kemmi instructed. She looked into a large microscope.

"Yes, ma'am. Pardon me, Gwin," I said, placing a hand on his body. Curses left a dark red crest on the body wherever they had been inflicted. I didn't know why, but I could dispel hexes by concentrating darkness toward that spot.

I pulled back Gwin's clothes, and my breath caught in my throat.

"..."

The dark red crest had expanded from his right arm to cover nearly his entire body. Only the extremities of his left arm and left leg retained their original color.

I can't believe it's this bad..., I thought, speechless. "H-hey, Chairwoman Kemmi... Do you think I can actually save him?"

Gwin extended his left hand, which still had some mobility, toward me. His breathing grew labored from the effort. I grabbed it and gave a reassuring squeeze.

"It's okay. I'm going to heal you!" I promised him.

My darkness was able to repel even demonic curses. Monsters were lower creatures, so no matter how bad this man's symptoms were, I should be able to heal him.

"I'm going to get started," I said.

I concentrated and cloaked Gwin's entire body in darkness. I did so gently, with the intention of wiping away the evil presence in his body, and his dark red skin returned to its original clear color before my eyes.

"Wow…!" Kemmi gasped excitedly while observing through her equipment.

I glanced at her and then addressed Gwin. "I successfully dispelled the curse. How do you feel?"

"I-I can move… I can move again!" he cried, moving his right arm slowly while remaining on the examination table.

…He can't stand yet. That's not surprising. His muscles had surely atrophied after decades of being bedridden. He would have to go through physical therapy to rebuild strength in his muscles.

"Ha-ha… This is incredible! I can move my arms, fingers, and feet, too!" he shouted.

But Gwin didn't seem to care that he wouldn't be able to walk immediately. His great joy was plain to see.

"Hmm, very intriguing…" Kemmi removed her eye from the microscope and thought.

"Did you figure anything out?" I asked.

"No, not yet. But I saw something very interesting."

"What's that?"

"When you dispelled the curse, it almost looked as if the dark red crest destroyed itself in order to avoid your darkness… Very interesting indeed. For the next round, I'm going to use a different device to more closely study the reaction of the patient's skin cells," she said, beginning to operate a different machine. She addressed the two holy knights. "Can you please bring in the next patient?"

""Yes, ma'am!""

They walked toward Gwin's stretcher to take him out of the room.

"W-wait!" the man cried.

"What is it, Gwin? Do you still feel pain?" I asked.

"No, I feel fine. I just... Could you please tell me your name, sir?!" he asked with burning intensity.

"U-uhh... It's Allen Rodol," I responded.

"Allen Rodol, yes?! I will never forget that name as long as I live! You're a wonderful young man... Thank you so much!" Gwin thanked me from the bottom of his heart. He had suffered for so long.

"I'm so glad I was able to heal you. Good luck with physical therapy."

"Thank you! I owe you more than words can express. I promise I'll pay you back some day!"

"I'll look forward to it."

The holy knights carried Gwin, now fully healed, out of the room.

■

The research progressed at a fast pace after I healed Gwin. The holy knights carried one patient into the room after another, and I dispelled each of their hexes in seconds with my darkness. Kemmi used a number of different instruments to analyze the gloom and the curses from every possible angle.

I ended up healing over a thousand curse victims in the first day in about eighteen hours of work—a rate of one patient per minute. My stamina was holding up just fine, but I was feeling the strain on my spirit power. It wouldn't be a problem, though; I felt like I could do this for another week.

We learned two major things from the first day of research. First, that my darkness made no contact with the curses. Second, the dark red seals destroyed themselves once they came within three centimeters of the darkness. Kemmi's hypothesis was that the gloom contained some component that the hexes could not withstand.

On the second day of the project, we were flooded with patients from Polyesta and Ronzo. The empress had announced to the world that Liengard had found a cure for curses through independent research. I devoted myself to healing all the patients who were placed before me, and Kemmi observed them with care.

Unfortunately, our efforts brought no progress toward a cure. Kemmi spent the entire day analyzing the components of the darkness, but she didn't figure anything out. It seemed like modern scientific equipment wasn't capable of revealing the secret of the darkness, and the research came to a standstill.

Day three of the Curse Cure Research Project arrived, and we were feeling the heat. This was the day that Kemmi's debt was due—once the clock struck midnight, her home would be seized.

Not that I care about that. She only has herself to blame for getting into debt.

More importantly, many would die if we didn't find a cure imminently. Feeling a strong sense of impatience, I focused on the only thing I could do—dispelling the curses before me.

When the clock struck eight at night, Kemmi tore at her hair and screamed.

"ARRGGHH! No, no, no! That's all wrong! Damn it, why can't I find it…?"

It was looking like another day of zero progress.

"Are you doing okay, Allen? Do you need a break?" Lia asked.

"Thanks Lia, but I'm fine. I can keep going," I said. A few seconds later, two holy knights opened the door and walked in with another patient.

"This is Ohrot Drasten. He is seventy-one years old and suffering from the Paralysis Curse, which numbs a part of the body and renders it unable to move," one of them explained.

"He was hexed last fall at seventy years old after being bitten by a monster while traveling from Aurest to Drestia. His right arm is totally immobilized," the other holy knight continued.

I treated it straight away after the holy knights finished their report.

"Your right arm was bitten, correct? Pardon me," I said as I lifted his limp right hand.

"H-huh?! Amazing! I can move it again!" he exclaimed.

"What...?" I responded, confused. Ohrot waved around his previously immobile right arm.

"You're incredible, sir! You healed my curse so quickly! You might be humanity's hope!" he said.

"I, uh..."

I hadn't done anything yet. I summoned no darkness to heal him; the curse simply dispelled on its own.

"Allen... What did you just do?" Kemmi asked, her eyes wide with astonishment.

"Nothing. I just touched his hand," I whispered, and she started muttering to herself.

"Interesting... I've had the wrong idea all along. My assumption that Allen's darkness was healing the curses sent me down the wrong path... I shouldn't be analyzing the curses or the darkness, but Allen's body!" She lifted her head, looking newly energized. "Allen! Next time, touch the dark red crest without using any darkness! I might have just had a breakthrough!"

"Yes, ma'am!"

The holy knights brought the next patient in right away. This time, I touched their dark red crest without using any gloom. I watched to see what would happen.

"I-it disappeared?!" I said, shocked. The crest that symbolized the curse had vanished. "What does this mean?!"

"It means everything! I've cracked it, Allen! It's not the darkness that the curses are avoiding—it's *you*. The only reason they vanish when the gloom approaches is because it's connected to you!" Kemmi gushed excitedly, jumping to her feet. "I know exactly what to do! Wait one moment!"

She dashed out of the room and returned with test tubes, beakers, and a bunch of different drugs in hand.

"All right, Allen! I'm gonna study that mysterious body of yours inside and out!"

"Okay!"

Kemmi extracted cells from my body and studied them in silence. It appeared as if we had finally stumbled upon the clue we needed to develop the cure for curses.

■

Kemmi didn't look up from her research for another hour.

"Heh-heh-heh... Ha-ha-ha! Heck yeah! I've finally found it!" she yelled triumphantly, lifting a test tube into the air.

"Do you mean...?!"

"A cure for curses...?!"

Kemmi nodded vigorously in response to me and Lia's questions.

"You bet! I used a number of reagents on Allen's cells and found a special cell that normal humans don't have! Hmm... I'll call it the Allen Cell out of convenience," she said. She looked happy enough to dance about her big discovery. "I started testing the Allen Cell once I was sure it was the answer. Then I applied it to a small sample of skin tissue from a cursed patient, and it worked like a dream! The curse disappeared in an instant!"

Her enthusiasm was something to behold.

"And the new medicine I made derived from the Allen Cell is...right here!" Kemmi declared, pointing at an ointment on the desk. "This is the first prototype of a treatment I made by combining anti-inflammatory components with the Allen Cell! Let's call in the next patient and see how it works!"

"Y-you're testing it on someone already?!" I asked.

"Ah-ha-ha, it'll be okay. I've already confirmed that the Allen Cell is harmless by testing it on human skin tissue. The chances of it having a negative effect on the patient are slim to none!" Kemmi assured, looking at a large number of microscope slides on the desk. She had already confirmed the safety of the medicine.

"Oh, that's good," I said. It was sure to be safe if the world's best medical doctor displayed that level of confidence in it.

"Heh-heh, we're on the brink of the discovery of the century! Bring in the next patient, please!" Kemmi requested.

The holy knights carried in the next curse victim, an eighty-five-year-old man named Harold Larsen. He suffered from the Fatigue Curse, which gave him an intense feeling of weariness around the clock. The holy knights said it was the result of a monster bite he'd sustained to his left leg two years ago.

"Pardon me," I said, using a long cotton swab to scoop out some of the prototype medicine and apply it to his discolored left leg. The dark red crest disappeared instantly, restoring his skin to normal.

Awesome, it works! It looked like the curse had been lifted completely. Now we just had to check to see if his fatigue was gone.

"How do you feel?" I asked nervously.

"Wow, I can't believe this! The sluggish feeling in my body is totally gone!" Harold said with an energetic smile.

"Really? That's great!"

The first prototype of the medicine using the Allen Cell was effective against curses; the research was a huge success.

The holy knights carried Harold out of the room.

"Woo-hoo! We've finally found a cure for curses! This is a massive discovery, one for the history books!" Kemmi said in celebration, waving her arms about like a child.

"Good job, Chairwoman Kemmi!" I said.

"Congratulations, Chairwoman Kemmi!" Lia added.

"Thank you! Medical science has taken a major step forward today! I couldn't have done it without your cooperation!"

We all high-fived, reveling in our joy.

"All right, let's hurry and report to Her Majesty! We can use this to save a lot of lives!" I said, standing up to dash out of the room.

"W-wait!" Kemmi suddenly cried out.

"Huh? What is it?" I asked.

"...Allen. We need to talk about this."

I had never seen her so serious before. *Talk about what?* I gulped, and a few seconds later she said something I couldn't fathom.

"We should tell the empress that our research was a failure," she said.

"Huh...?"

I was totally lost. We'd succeeded in developing a cure. Humanity finally had what it needed to defeat curses. Why would we say that we failed?

"Well, to be blunt... You can make a lot of money out of pharmaceuticals. If I get a patent on a new medicine using the Allen Cell that can cure any curse, I'll rake in so much cash that a hundred million guld will be chump change!" Kemmi said with a dark smile. "This Curse Cure Research Project was funded by Liengard. According to the contract, any discoveries we make will belong to the empress. That means we'll lose the rights to the Allen Cell and the new medicine."

Kemmi pulled the pledge we signed for the Curse Cure Research Project out of her pocket.

"This means I'll only get a measly one hundred million guld for making the greatest discovery of our time... Hence why we should pretend that we failed. We can start a new research project together in a few days and coincidentally discover the Allen Cell then. That way, the rights to the new medicine will be all mi—whoops, sorry! They'll belong to both of us. We'll be swimming in guld! Let's see... Would you be satisfied with seventy percent of the profits for me and thirty for you?"

Holy crap...

This was sickening. She would turn a blind eye to over a hundred thousand lives for her own profit. This woman was rotten to the core. I couldn't even fathom the greed it would take to not be satisfied with one hundred million guld under these circumstances. No wonder Idora and the other White Lily students were so sick of her.

"...Chairwoman Kemmi," I began.

"Yes, Allen?!" she responded.

"I'll hear no more of this nonsense. We're giving Her Majesty an honest report right now."

This new medicine was the hope that all the curse victims in the world had been waiting for. If Kemmi patented the Allen Cell, she would sell it for an exorbitant price out of the sole interest of lining her pockets. I couldn't let that happen.

"Grk... Okay, fine. I suppose I was greedy to ask for seventy percent considering your great contribution to this project. How about a sixty-forty split?!"

She really didn't get it.

"Let's go talk to Her Majesty, Lia," I said.

"Yeah, let's go!" Lia responded.

"H-hey, wait! I'll go half and half! You can have fifty percent of the profits!" Kemmi shouted.

I ignored her and dragged her to the palace as she tried every trick in the book to win me over.

■

Lia, Kemmi, and I went to Liengard Palace and reported to the empress about the Allen Cell and our new cure for curses. The empress ordered the new medicine to be mass-produced as quickly as possible and promised that it would be exported to Polyesta and Ronzo for a cheap price. Kemmi reluctantly accepted her payment of one hundred million guld and paid off the debt collector, while Lia and I returned to our dorm for the first time in a few days.

Lia and I spent the last two days of our winter break doing New Year's activities like visiting shrines and stocking up on grocery specials. It was a relaxing change of pace.

I wanted to visit Mom and Ms. Paula, but that didn't work out. Lia wasn't feeling well on account of staying up for two nights straight as we searched for a cure for curses. *Goza Village is pretty far away. I can't take Lia along if she feels sick, but I can't leave her behind, either.* I regretfully postponed those trips until spring break at the earliest.

January 7 arrived, marking the end of our two-week break and the resumption of our Thousand Blade classes.

"Ngh... The weather seems nice," I said, rousing to warm sunlight streaming through the curtains. It was seven in the morning, a perfect time to wake up.

Where's Lia...? Oh, she's over there. Enticing smells were coming from the kitchen; she must have been making breakfast.

"Good morning, Lia. Do you feel okay?" I asked.

"Oh, good morning Allen. I feel great. Thanks for asking," Lia responded.

"That's good to hear."

I got out of bed, ate a delicious breakfast, got dressed quickly, and left for Thousand Blade with Lia. Once we reached Class 1-A, I opened the door and saw Tessa and the rest of my classmates.

"Good morning, everyone," I said. I hadn't seen them in two weeks.

"Hey, you're finally here!"

"You're in the newspaper, Allen! Looks like you were up to your usual heroics again!"

"Allen, was the demon as strong as they say? I've heard the holy knights in the palace were knocked out without a fight..."

"What's this 'Allen Cell' thing? The empress called it a wonder drug for curses... Were you involved with that, too?"

My classmates peppered me with rapid-fire questions. The government had released its restriction on information on January 3, so now everyone knew about the demon attack.

"U-umm..."

I answered them one by one until the *ding-dong-ding-dong* of the bell announced the start of homeroom. The door flew open, and Chairwoman Reia entered the classroom.

"Good morning, boys and girls! It's time to start homeroom!" she said before diving into an announcement with her usual pep. She said Claude had made a temporary return to Vesteria to attend an important meeting as captain of Lia's personal guard.

"Okay, that does it for announcements. I'd like to move right on to first period, but there's something else I need to say first," Chairwoman Reia said. She looked at me. "I heard about how you distinguished yourself fighting off that demon, Allen! The empress had high praise for you!"

"U-uhh...," I responded blankly, caught off guard by the change of topic.

"An attack on Liengard Palace is completely unprecedented. I wanted to be there to help, but the other Thousand Blade teachers and I were on a company trip in Cherin, the Land of Sakura. I was totally stuck... You have my apologies."

"No, don't blame yourself. No one could have predicted that would happen."

This was the first time in Liengard's long history that the imperial residence had been attacked, and it had happened out of nowhere. It was ridiculous to expect anyone to be ready for something like that. There was nothing wrong with the chairwoman going on the New Year's company trip—even *she* needed breaks.

"Hearing you say that makes me feel a little better. You did something truly incredible, Allen. It makes me proud to be the chairwoman of Thousand Blade!" Reia said, patting me on the back. "Okay, that's all I had to say. First and second period will be our first Soul Attire classes of the new year—let's get off to a good start!"

""""Yes, ma'am!"""""

■

After we moved to the Soul Attire room, I focused on starting a dialogue with my Spirit Core. There wasn't a single student holding a soul-crystal sword. We could now enter the Soul World unassisted.

Okay, let's get started. I closed my eyes and plunged my consciousness into the depths of my soul. When I opened my eyes, I saw a desolate world. Rotten vegetation, ruined soil, stagnant air. That irksome, dry landscape extended as far as the eye could see.

I looked up at a tall boulder and saw *him* sitting upon it, wearing a vicious expression.

"Hey. It's been a while since we were last face-to-face," I said.

"...Oh, it's the brat. Did you miss gettin' the shit kicked outta you?" my Spirit Core responded, slowly getting to his feet. He summoned an eerily black sword, and a spine-chilling malice seemed to engulf our surroundings. Though he looked ready to fight, that wasn't what I had in mind.

"Wait, that's not why I'm here. I just want to talk!" I clarified quickly.

"Huh? You want to *talk*?" he repeated.

"Yeah. We don't have to fight every time we see each other."

He clicked his tongue loudly and sat back down on his boulder. "*Tch.* This better not be boring, or I *will* kill you."

I hadn't expected him to relent so easily.

"I want to confirm something first... Your name is Zeon, right?" I asked.

"Duh. You call your Spirit Core's name, and I lend you my strength—that's how Soul Attire works," he answered bluntly, glaring at me.

He might've agreed to talk, but I can't expect him to be friendly... I needed to get my questions out before his mood worsened any further.

"So, Zeon, what's the darkness of the Rodol Clan that Seele Grazalio was talking about? Is it different from the kind you wield?"

"...What you have is my darkness, through and through," he responded vaguely after a short pause.

He's hiding something... It wasn't like Zeon to be so guarded. He was clearly a bad liar. *I don't think pursuing that topic any further will get him to answer honestly, though.* There was a secret related to the darkness, and it was important enough for Zeon to want to hide it from me. That alone was valuable information.

He has an incredibly short temper, so I shouldn't press him too hard on any one question. I'll go on to the next one before he can get angry, I decided.

"Why did Seele know about you? Have you met before?"

"How should I know? I'd never remember a weak-ass demon like him," Zeon said. His answer was immediate this time. It appeared there was a clear line between what he could tell me and what he couldn't.

"I see..."

He really didn't seem to know anything about the demon. *So Seele is aware of him, but not the other way around... Is Zeon a celebrity Spirit Core among the demons or something?"*

"Hey, I got somethin' to ask you," Zeon said. It was rare for him to drive the conversation.

"S-sure, ask me anything," I replied, surprised.

"When are you gonna stop bein' so complacent, you little brat?"

"Huh?"

I wasn't sure what he meant.

"You worked your ass off to steal a small sliver of my power... So why won't you even try to use it?"

"Uh, but I've been using your darkness and the black sword."

"Huh... Are you sick in the head? Open those peepers of yours and see the true nature of my power. You're gonna cause problems for me if you don't grow, got it?!"

"?!"

Zeon yelled, and I stepped back on instinct just as a black slash passed where my head had been.

Man, that was close! If I had reacted a split second later, I would've been finished.

"That's enough of this stupid conversation. Draw your sword if you wanna last longer than two seconds," Zeon said, suddenly clutching his black blade. He was going to force me to fight.

"Damn it, guess this was bound to happen…," I muttered as I brought my hand into the air. "Destroy—Rapacious Demon Zeon." I grabbed the same ebon sword as him. "Okay… Are you ready?"

"Of course I'm goddamn ready! I'm gonna slaughter you dead!"

Zeon and I began the first duel we'd had in a while.

■

I assumed the middle stance. Zeon dangled his sword listlessly, as per usual. *He looks totally defenseless, but his reflexes are absurd.* He'd cut me down immediately if I charged at him without a plan. I would have to close the distance using my usual method.

"First Style—Flying Shadow!"

I quickly swung my sword three times, sending a trio of black slashes his way. Probing moves were useless against him. I had to rely on my strongest attacks and hope I could land a hit.

The three arcs raced straight for Zeon, tearing up the dry ground. I hid behind one of them so he wouldn't be able to follow my exact position as I approached.

"Hah, you're still usin' that same trick? How basic… Yah!" Zeon sneered and knocked aside the three slashes with his left hand.

He's ridiculously strong! I can't help but be impressed.

With the Flying Shadows gone, our gazes met.

"Eighth Style—Eight-Span Crow!" I shouted, and eight tremendously powerful projectiles closed in on him. I released two of them low so they would tear up the ground. Those two slashes kicked up dry sand, clouding Zeon's vision.

"Why, you little...!"

Shutting his right eye, he swung his blade horizontally, dispelling both the arcs and the sand.

Now!

Zeon's visibility was limited because he was squinting, so I snuck over to his right side and unleashed my fastest attack.

"Seventh Style—Draw Flash!" I yelled, slicing his right shoulder with a draw flash surpassing the speed of sound. *I got him! Heck yeah!*

"Oh, was that you? I thought it was a bugbite," he taunted before counterattacking without hesitation.

Are you kidding me?!

I quickly stepped back and dodged by a paper-thin margin.

"Hah. Only amateurs resort to crude ploys like blinding your opponent," Zeon said. He focused darkness onto his right shoulder and healed his wound instantly.

"I'm self-taught. That simplicity is one of my strengths," I responded. My style of fighting was free, not beholden to any form or tradition. That was one of the few advantages of being self-taught.

"Well, I guess it's a little better than some boring, run-of-the-mill style, but...you're gonna need better swordcraft to overcome my massive strength advantage."

Zeon cracked his neck and summoned ten dark tentacles that rose from his body.

Is that Dark Shadow?!

I responded by using Dark Shadow and summoning ten tentacles of my own.

"Heh, you've matched my number of tendrils... Let's see what good that does you!" Zeon shouted.

I used Dark Shadow and the black sword to attack Zeon with desperate intensity. I gave everything I had, utilizing all my skills in the hope that I would have even a small chance of victory—but ended up suffering a miserable defeat.

"*Haah, haah...*" I gasped for air as I lay on my back, still gripping my broken black sword. *Damn it... I hate to admit it, but he's ridiculously strong.*

Zeon's darkness was as sharp as a blade, as soft as water, and as hard as steel. And that wasn't all—its form was ever-changing. It could be as elastic as rubber, as sticky as melted candy, or as scorching as the sun. I had known his darkness's power far surpassed mine, but I didn't realize he was this much more proficient with it as well.

"Good lord... You're so weak I almost feel like I could cry. Can't you do any better than that?" Zeon spat, smiling after winning in dominant fashion.

He pisses me off, but I can learn a lot from him... Zeon had just showed how he could alter the form of his darkness. That was a very useful skill. It peeved me to imitate him, but I was going to practice it later. Each time he and I clashed, I felt like I came out a little stronger, slightly narrowing the gap between me and him. I couldn't imagine a better feeling.

I don't think...I can stay awake much longer... As my consciousness faded, I used the last of my strength to hold up three fingers.

"Huh? What does that mean?" Zeon asked.

"Three times... I've never cut you three times before!" I said.

"Why're you so proud of barely grazing my skin, dweeb?"

"Because I had never managed to cut you more than once in a fight until now... I've gotten a *little* stronger, haven't I?"

"Yeah, you're at least as powerful as a gnat now."

"Hah, surely I'm better than that... Well, just you watch... I *will* surpass you..."

All I could do was stay the course. If I grew a little stronger every day, I would overtake this monster eventually.

"Hmph. I'll give you a little hint outta respect for your wasted effort. This darkness both belongs to me and doesn't."

"What do you—"

"Use that puny brain of yours to puzzle it out!"

He swung his black sword down and my vision went white. My consciousness returned to the real world.

■

After our Soul Attire classes in first and second period ended, I headed for the Student Council room with Lia and Rose. We were going to attend the first regular meeting—which was really nothing more than a casual lunch—of the year.

"I haven't seen Shii, Lilim, and Tirith in a couple weeks," I said.

"Yeah, I'm excited to hang out with them," Lia responded.

"Ha-ha, me too," Rose agreed.

We continued to chat until we arrived at the Student Council room. I knocked on the door.

"I-is that Allen?!"

Lilim swung open the door in a panic.

"Y-yeah, it's me. What's the matter?" I asked.

"It's terrible, Allen! I don't know what to do!" Lilim yelled, grabbing my by the shoulders and rocking me back and forth. I didn't know what happened, but she was clearly distraught.

"P-please calm down... Let's go inside," I said, knowing this conversation wasn't going to get anywhere unless I interrupted her.

I entered the room and saw Tirith slumped on the couch in low spirits. *Whatever happened, it must be really bad if she looks that down...*

I motioned for Lilim to sit on the couch. "So, what's this all about?" I asked.

"Shii dropped out of Thousand Blade...," Lilim revealed.

"...Huh?" It took me a second to process what I heard.

"A-are you kidding?!" Lia shouted.

"What made her do that?!" Rose asked.

The two of them were both visibly shaken as well.

"Our homeroom teacher couldn't have been clearer... Shii is leaving Thousand Blade Academy, effective today," Lilim continued, sounding like she could burst into tears at any moment.

"That doesn't make sense... Are you sure there hasn't been some mistake?" I asked.

Lilim shook her head. "Shii's room is empty. She already moved out of the dorm..."

"No way..."

An oppressive feeling settled over the Student Council room.

The last time I saw Shii was at the New Year's Jubilee. She was her usual self that day. That means something happened between the first and seventh of the month. Something terrible enough to make her drop out of Thousand Blade.

"Well, let's go find out what happened," I said.

"Who would we ask?" Lilim wondered.

"Chairwoman Reia, of course," I responded. As the head of Thousand Blade Academy, she had to know what was going on with her students. "Okay, let's go."

The five of us left the room and went to her office.

■

I knocked three quick times on the black door of the chair's office.

"Come in," Chairwoman Reia called out stiffly.

"Excuse us," I said as we entered.

"Oh, it's you all," she said, glancing up at us from her desk.

I spoke up for the group. "Chairwoman, is it true that Shii dropped out of Thousand Blade Academy?"

"...Yeah. She filled out the paperwork to withdraw two days ago," she answered.

"............"

We were all shocked and speechless at the terrible truth. Shii really had dropped out. And she'd done so without telling anybody.

"Can you tell us why?!" Lilim pleaded.

"I find it very unlikely that Shii did this of her own accord...!" Tirith added.

They both looked desperate for answers. Lilim and Tirith had known Shii better than us, and they were clearly in disbelief at this turn of events.

Tirith's exactly right. Shii always seemed like she was having fun. She used her position as Student Council president to enjoy her time here more than anyone else. It was difficult to believe she had dropped out willingly.

"...I'm not in a position to discuss this matter," Reia answered.

If she couldn't comment on it as the chairwoman of Thousand Blade, that could only mean one thing.

"Is the government involved?" I pressed, and she averted her gaze and went quiet. Her silence spoke volumes; it seemed like the Liengardian government really had forced Shii to drop out of Thousand Blade.

"...I'm sorry. There's nothing I can do about it," Chairwoman Reia said. She got up and walked through us toward the door.

"Please wait! Where are you going?!" I protested.

"Don't try to avoid us, Reia!" Lia said.

The chairwoman suddenly stopped and searched the inside of her jacket. "Whoops, I misplaced the top-secret document I got from Her Majesty. I'd lose my head if that leaked, but...I'm too hungry to worry about that right now. I'm gonna take a *nice, long lunch*, and search my desk thoroughly when I get back," she said exaggeratedly, and left the office.

■

We all glanced at each other after Chairwoman Reia left the room. "*I misplaced the top-secret document I got from her Majesty. I'm gonna take a* nice, long lunch. *Search my desk thoroughly.*" She'd indirectly told us to look through her desk while she was away.

As an Elite Five Academy chair, she can't openly object to whatever happened. But that didn't mean she was on board with it. Thank you so much, Chairwoman Reia!

I quickly started fishing through her desk. A few minutes later, I found a document labeled "Top Secret" buried deep in a completely unorganized drawer.

"Th-this is it!" I said.

"Good job, Allen!" Lilim cheered.

"Let's read it...!" Tirith urged.

I put the document on the desk, and we all leaned forward intently to look it over. We couldn't believe our eyes.

"A political marriage...?" I said.

The document outlined a plan to marry Shii Arkstoria, the eldest daughter of the Arkstoria family, to a high-ranking noble from the Holy Ronelian Empire named Numelo Dohran. The goal of the marriage was to improve Liengard's relationship with Ronelia and postpone war between the two nations a little while. The government was marrying Shii off just to save some time.

"I've heard of Numelo Dohran!" Lilim exclaimed.

"He's that man from Ronelia who's courted Shii for years...," Tirith added.

They both looked grim.

"It doesn't get much worse than House Dohran...," Lia said with disgust.

"Do you know something about them, Lia?" I asked.

"Yeah... House Dohran is a major noble family in the Holy Ronelian Empire that controls the mining industry. They've gained enormous wealth from selling soul crystals and blood diamonds for extremely high prices." Lia seemed to search through her memory as she spoke. "There was a conference a few years ago between Vesteria and Ronelia. I saw Numelo Dohran there. He's a portly man with greedy eyes...and I've heard he treats women like playthings."

"«««««   »»»»»»
 ..."

That last anecdote dashed our spirits even more.

"So basically, Liengard sold Shii to Ronelia in the hopes of slightly delaying the war," Rose said, seething with anger.

"That doesn't make sense! Her father is *so* overprotective of her! There's no way he'd allow it!" Lilim yelled.

"I want to go see her dad and ask him about this…!" Tirith insisted.

They're exactly right, I thought. Rodis doted on his daughter like nobody's business. It was impossible to believe he would just sit back and let this political marriage happen. *He wouldn't care if he had orders from above, or if he couldn't reject the marriage as a member of the Arkstoria family. He would save his daughter by any means necessary.*

"That's worth a shot," I agreed.

"Let's go!" Lilim said.

"This is hardly the time to worry about classes…!" Tirith added.

We left Chairwoman Reia's office to go speak to Shii's father, Rodis Arkstoria.

■

We decided to skip third period and beyond to go to the Arkstoria mansion. *I haven't been here since the summer training camp…* I never imagined I would come back here in such a low mood.

I knocked on the grand door, and a few moments later, Rodis Arkstoria appeared.

"It's Allen Rodol…and Shii's friends," he said, glaring at me as if I was his sworn enemy.

"Hello, Mr. Rodis. Could we have a little of your time?" I asked.

"Sorry, but I'm busy. Come back another day," Rodis said gruffly. He tried to close the door, but Rose put her foot in the entrance to stop him. Her quick decision-making never failed to impress.

I quickly told Rodis what we were here for so as to not waste the time

Rose had bought for us. "We want to talk about how the Presiden—er, Shii dropped out of Thousand Blade. It's important."

"That's a family matter. My daughter decided to study abroad to further develop her swordcraft. It's none of your business. Go back to school," he responded, refusing to let us in. Realizing this wasn't going anywhere, I decided to reveal what we knew.

"Shii is being married off to Numelo Dohran," I said.

Rodis's eyebrows twitched. "How do you know about that...?" he asked, furious. Unsurprisingly, it looked like he didn't approve of the political marriage in the slightest.

"All that matters is that we do. Would you be willing to talk to us, Mr. Rodis?" I asked.

"...Come inside," he said curtly, opening the door.

■

We entered the Arkstoria mansion and followed Rodis down a long hallway.

The Arkstoria family's wealth is astounding..., I thought, marveling at the luxurious red carpet on the floor and the paintings on the walls.

"We'll talk in here," he said, opening a door and inviting us in. It was a simple living room furnished with two large black couches and an elegant wooden table in between. Judging by its modesty, I assumed it was only a place to talk.

"Please sit," he said, plunking down onto the couch on the far end of the room. I thanked him and sat on the sofa opposite him. "Where did you learn about the political marriage, Allen Rodol? That's a state secret."

Rodis looked at me sharply as if interrogating me.

"We can't reveal our source," I responded. Chairwoman Reia could lose her job if we said her name here. That was no way to repay the favor she'd given us.

"Hmph. Very well. So, what do you want?" he asked.

"We want to talk about Sh—," I began, but Lilim interrupted me, unable to contain herself any longer.

"How can you be so calm, Mr. Rodis?! Shii's gonna end up in the clutches of that gross Numelo guy if we don't do anything! Are you really okay with that?!" she yelled.

"OF COURSE NOT!" he yelled thunderously, swinging his fist down onto the table and breaking it clean in half, sending sawdust into the air. "Do you really think I could let that despicable man lay his hands on my darling daughter?! I'm going to Ronelia to sabotage the wedding ceremony!"

It seemed like Rodis had only been acting cool earlier; it must've been difficult keeping himself together.

The room fell silent, and I asked a question. "How do you plan to get to Ronelia? Everyone knows you can't get there by plane or boat."

Liengard had forbidden travel to the holy empire. You couldn't get there by public air or sea routes.

"That's not an issue. I'm going to use Dodriel Barton's Shadow Traversal ability to send myself there," Rodis answered.

""""What?!""""

Lia, Rose, and I were shocked to hear that name.

"This isn't known to the general public, but a swordsman named Dodriel has placed shadows in various points on land and sea that you can use to instantly travel from one place to another. We call them shadow spots," Rodis said. It sounded like Dodriel had been busy. "I've learned the location of the shadow spot that leads directly into Ronelia. Getting into the country will be easy."

"...I see," I said. He was going to infiltrate Ronelia via shadow spot, and then use it again to come home with Shii. "But where did you learn about this?"

"Where do you think? I consulted the expert on all things underworld."

"Do you mean...Ms. Rize?"

"Yes. I pulled some strings and forced the Blood Fox into a meeting with me. There really is no limit to that woman's knowledge. She took half of my personal worth as payment for the info, but…it was the last piece I needed to get Shii back."

Rodis clenched his fists tightly. There was a burning intensity in his eyes. Lia and Rose, who had been silent until now, asked questions in succession.

"Isn't charging into the middle of enemy territory on your own way too reckless?" Lia asked.

"And won't Ronelia retaliate if the head of the Arkstoria family does something so drastic?" Rose followed.

"I'm fully aware of how risky this is. But there's nothing to fear. I won't leave any evidence that I was the assailant. I'm going to wear those around my stomach to make sure of that," Rodis answered, glancing at a ring-shaped strap of bombs.

""""""What?!""""""

"Those are all custom-made explosives created by a Soul-Attire wielder I know. They're powerful enough to erase anyone killed from their blasts without a trace. If I fail to rescue Shii, I'll detonate the bombs immediately so that no one will be able to identify me. If I succeed, I'll have no need for them. Honor is more important to a noble than their own life. Numelo will do anything to cover up the shame of a single person stealing his bride away. So whether I succeed or fail, Liengard and Ronelia will maintain their amicable relationship on the surface. I won't cause any inconvenience for Her Majesty," he explained further. He spoke of his own death with shocking indifference.

"I don't understand… Why would you go so far to protect the empress?!" I asked.

I couldn't make sense of it. I was sure there were complicated political and diplomatic circumstances at play, but the empress had essentially sold Shii to Ronelia. She'd used Rodis's beloved daughter as a bargaining chip. What could possibly compel him to continue serving her?

"Tradition. We Arkstorias have defended the empress's family for generations. I cannot spit on centuries of service," Rodis answered gravely, closing his eyes.

Centuries, huh... As someone who'd swung his sword tirelessly for over a billion years, a couple hundred felt like the blink of an eye. To normal people, however, that was quite a long time.

"Also, Her Majesty deserves no blame for this matter. She is simply doing her best to help our nation recover. The true object of our hatred should be that insufferable—no, I should say no more..." Rodis halted, grinding his back teeth.

The empress deserves no blame...? Something about his wording bothered me.

"I don't really get all this complicated stuff, but I'll help! I'll go to the empire or even the depths of hell to save Shii!" Lilim declared, jumping to her feet.

"Shii's my best friend... I'm coming, too...!" Tirith said, doing the same.

"No, you're not. This is an Arkstoria family matter. I will not involve outsiders," Rodis refused curtly. He got up and opened the door to the living room. "We're done here. I need to prepare for battle and ready my spirit power. If you truly care about Shii, pray for the success of my operation and go back to school."

""..."""

If you truly care about Shii. Lilim and Tirith had to grit their teeth and nod after hearing that.

"...Let's go, everyone," Lilim said.

"...It looks like there's nothing we can do," Tirith added.

They both trudged out of the room, looking depressed.

"Hey, wait up, you two!" I called out.

Lia, Rose, and I hurried after them. We plodded back down the hallway in low spirits and left through the front door.

"Thank you. Shii is blessed to have great friends like all of you," Rodis said before we left, giving us a clumsy smile.

■

We returned to the Student Council room after leaving the Arkstoria mansion.

«««««　»»»»»»
...

The room felt even gloomier than before. The ticking of the clock was uncomfortably loud.

"Urgh, Shii...," Lilim moaned.

"This is so terrible...," Tirith mumbled, sounding numb.

The two of them hadn't met Shii at Thousand Blade Academy—they were all childhood friends. The length of their friendship was making this all the more painful for them. I couldn't imagine how they felt.

Damn it, is there nothing we can do?

I wanted to save Shii, too. It pained me to think that I would never get to see her again, without even having an opportunity to say goodbye. But this was a complicated situation. The empress was trying to protect Liengard. Rodis was prepared to sacrifice himself for his daughter. And most importantly, Shii had chosen to obey and go to the Holy Ronelian Empire alone. We could easily end up making the situation worse if we did the wrong thing.

If only I had an idea about what Shii really wants. How she really feels...

Things would have been so much simpler if I knew whether Shii wanted me to save her, or if she wanted me to do nothing. I couldn't take action without that knowledge.

President..., I thought, looking at her unoccupied desk. *Huh?* I noticed that the drawer was slightly ajar. Curious, I grabbed the handle and pulled it open to look inside. There was an envelope in there.

"What's this?" I said aloud. There was cute, girly handwriting on the back saying *To the Student Council*. "It's a note from Shii..."

Lilim and Tirith ran toward me.

"A note from Shii...?!" Lilim asked.

"R-really...?!" Tirith pressed.

Lia and Rose also rushed over.

"What does it say?!" Lia asked.

"Go ahead and read it, Allen!" Rose urged.

I opened the envelope and read the letter inside out loud.

"By the time you read this letter, I will have left Thousand Blade. I'm sorry for dropping out without saying anything. Certain circumstances beyond my control are forcing me out of the country," I read.

She hadn't intended on telling us about the political marriage.

"Lilim, Tirith. Thank you for putting up with all my selfish whims. My school life was a blast thanks to you two. I would be very happy if you kept me in your memories," I continued.

"Sh-Shii...," Lilim said, beginning to cry.

"How could we ever forget about you...?" Tirith asked, biting her bottom lip.

"Lia, Rose. You two breathed new life into the Student Council. Thank you for always coming to the regular meetings. I can depart in peace knowing the Student Council has two such reliable girls to support it. Lilim and Tirith...are just as prone to slacking off as I am, so I would appreciate it if you could help them out."

"Shii...," Lia muttered, her eyes welling up.

"Grk..." Rose balled her fists in frustration.

"And finally, Allen. You're a bully and I have nothing to say to you... Just kidding. We faced each other quite a few times, didn't we? The Club Budget War, poker, the Shadow Thousand Blade Festival, Christmas... And I lost on every single occasion. You're very strong, so I want you to protect everyone in my absence. That's my final request for you as your older sister."

Shii had been worried about us until the end.

"My days in the Student Council with you all were so much fun. Farewell."

The letter ended there. The final *farewell* was blotted, likely from a tear.

Shii...

The president came off as a self-centered person who was rarely honest about her feelings...but she was also hopelessly good-natured. *She has to be suffering more than we can imagine. She must want us to save her.* And yet, she'd never once asked for our help. Probably because she didn't want to burden us.

But there was one thing her letter conveyed, even if she hadn't put it into words. *I now know how she really feels.* The tears on the letter spoke volumes in that regard.

Oh yeah... I made a promise to her on Christmas. I said, "I'll come to your aid any time you ask for my help." Mom and Ms. Paula both taught me something important, too—that swordfighters should always keep their promises, even if it kills them.

"I've made up my mind. I'm going to save Shii," I declared.

I didn't care if I had to face the Holy Ronelian Empire or the Black Organization to do it. That couldn't matter less. If I didn't do something, the swordsman within me would die.

"I'm going, too! There's *no way* I'm gonna let my friendship with Shii end this way!" Lilim said, immediately giving her support.

"You're not leaving me behind...!" Tirith added.

Lia and Rose reacted with concern.

"Hold on, Allen! That's way too dangerous!" Lia protested.

"Lia's right. If this goes wrong, you could put not just Shii, but all of Liengard in danger!" Rose appealed. They both wanted me to rethink this.

"I'm aware of the risks. But do you remember what Rodis said? 'Honor is more important to a noble than their own life,'" I responded.

"«« »»"
...

Lia and Rose went quiet at my rebuttal.

"Numelo Dohran's reputation as a noble will be ruined if students like us manage to sabotage his wedding. He'll be desperate to cover it up," I continued.

If we successfully rescued Shii, Numelo would cover up the truth of what happened to protect his honor. He would do the same if we failed to prevent the wedding ceremony from being held. Either way, the amicable relationship Liengard and Ronelia maintained on the surface would persist, so there was no risk of causing trouble for Liengard.

"But Allen, how do you plan on getting into Ronelia? You can't enter the country by land or air. We don't know where Dodriel's shadow spots are, either," Lia asked.

"Well..."

Just as Lia had said, getting into the country was going to be very difficult. *Rodis claimed he knew the location of a shadow spot that leads directly into Ronelia. It would be easiest just to go there with him, but he insisted this was an Arkstoria family matter. I'm sure he'd reject us if we offered our help again.*

"Oh, I know! How about we ask the Blood Fox for help? That's how Rodis learned about the shadow spots!" Lilim proposed with an excited clap of her hands. She looked very proud of herself.

Lia, Rose, and Tirith shook their heads, however.

"I...don't think that's a good idea, Lilim," Lia said.

"Lia's right. Nothing good comes from involving yourself with her," Rose agreed.

"You need to make an appointment *months* in advance to meet with the Blood Fox anyway...," Tirith added.

"Oh, I should've known... Sorry. Forget about that...," Lilim responded, slumping in dejection.

"I was able to meet with her right away when I went to her mansion," I said.

Rize had agreed to see me immediately back when Lia was abducted by Zach Bombard and Tor Sammons. Things had been desperate, so we didn't have time to make an appointment.

Rose spoke up in response. "We should consider that a rare exception. I've heard that the Blood Fox even makes the empress wait a long time to meet with her. It's a miracle that Rodis was able to see her."

"R-really?" I asked, and the others nodded their agreement. It seemed like consulting Rize wouldn't be a realistic option.

We all brainstormed after that, but couldn't come up with any ideas. My impatience grew as more and more time passed with no progress.

Crap. Shii must be suffering right now, and we're not doing anything... I tightly balled my fists and searched my brain. Ronelia was pretty far from Liengard. Swimming there would be impossible. But it wasn't like we could take an airplane or a boat, either; no one would take a vessel to a country that Liengard had placed a travel ban on.

We really do need Dodriel's shadow spot. But even if we got lucky and found the one leading directly into the Holy Ronelian Empire, what would we do after that? We weren't at all familiar with Ronelian geography. Finding Numelo would be a difficult task. In other words, we needed to find someone who was knowledgeable of both Dodriel's shadow spots and the Ronelian map.

...Fat chance of that happening. The world wasn't so convenient a place. It was highly unlikely we would find someone with such a specific knowledge set.

Damn it. We're totally out of options..., I thought, gritting my teeth.

"Oh, it started raining," Lia muttered, looking out the window.

I strained my ears and heard a light pitter-patter of rain on the window. The sky was totally covered by clouds. It was the perfect reflection of our hopelessness.

It's raining... Oh, wait a second! The thought of rain made a lightbulb go off in my head. *I know someone who might be able to help!*

There was a single person who fit the criteria we needed. He was very familiar with the Holy Ronelian Empire and the Black Organization, and he might even know something about those shadow spots.

"Hey, why don't we ask *him*?!" I said.

""""...Who?"""""

"You know, that Oracle Knight! Raine Grad!"

"""...!"""

""Oracle Knight?!""

Lia and Rose looked stunned, while Lilim and Tirith's jaws dropped. The latter two were completely in the dark about him.

"Raine was a member of the Black Organization's senior management. He might know something about the spots!" I said.

The Black Organization's base of operations was in the Holy Ronelian Empire. Raine would absolutely be well-acquainted with the Ronelian landscape. There was even a chance he would know where a major noble like Numelo Dohran lived.

"H-hold on a second! Are you actually connected to the Black Organization, Allen?!" Lilim yelled.

"I'd heard the rumors, but I...I just couldn't believe it...!" Tirith said, just as shocked.

They both went pale and stepped back from me. It sounded like I'd inspired a terrible misunderstanding.

"No, you've got it all wrong! I just... Well, one thing led to another, and I ended up crossing blades with Raine," I clarified.

"You *fought* one of the Thirteen Oracle Knights?! What the heck... How did we not hear about such a major event?!" Lilim yelled, wide-eyed.

"When did you cross swords with him, and where?! I want to hear all about it...!" Tirith insisted.

"I'm sorry, but I'm not at liberty to tell you. I defeated Raine, though. You don't have to worry about that," I answered.

I'd promised Clown to keep my lips sealed about my expedition to Daglio. All I could say was that I'd won out over Raine.

"You *defeated* one of the Thirteen Oracle Knights?!" Lilim shouted.

"I suppose you did fight off that other Oracle Knight, Fuu Ludoras…," Tirith muttered.

They were both dumbfounded. Lia and Rose, who'd been with me when I fought Raine, considered my proposal.

"He hated the Black Organization, and he didn't seem like a bad person, either… There's definitely a chance he'll help us," Lia said.

"He was arrested by the holy knights, though. He's probably in prison somewhere. Do you have any idea how to find him, Allen?" Rose asked.

"Clown was closely involved with that case. He might be able to tell us something," I responded.

This sounded like a plan.

"I don't really get it, but we just have to go to the Holy Knights Association, right?!" Lilim asked.

"We have to try it, even if our chances are slim…!" Tirith insisted.

They both dashed out of the Student Council room.

"Let's go too, Lia and Rose!" I said.

"Okay!" Lia responded.

"Roger that!" Rose said.

And so we clung to this small hope of saving Shii and headed for the Holy Knights Association.

Afterword

Thank you very much to everyone who picked up the sixth volume of *100-Million-Year Button*!

I would like to start by briefly touching on the content of this novel. This will contain spoilers, so please be careful if you are the type to read the afterword first.

Volume 6 is comprised of three parts: the Christmas Party arc, the New Year's Jubilee arc, and the beginning of the Political Marriage arc.

The cuteness of the girls is on full display in the Christmas Party arc with Lia and Rose's Santa hats and Shii's Santa costume. I think this chapter turned out quite bright and fun on the whole.

Many new characters are introduced in the New Year's Jubilee arc, including the eccentric empress Wendy, the doting father Rodis Arkstoria, and the mysterious demon Seele Grazalio. They all have a meaningful impact and breathe new life into the story. The intense battle between Allen and Seele was a blast to write.

Shii is forced into an engagement at the beginning of the Political Marriage arc... And Allen and his friends decide to invade the Holy Ronelian Empire. The story moves on to the next volume as they stake their hopes on Raine Grad.

Volume 6 is a dense, action-packed novel! I'll be very happy if it brings even a little joy to my readers.

And Volume 7 is going to be amazing! A literal deluge of developments awaits, so please look forward to it! (I'm working hard on the manuscript!)

Volume 7 is scheduled to release in Japan in June, four months from now!

Now I'd like to give some words of thanks. To the illustrator Mokyu, the lead editor, the proofreader, and everyone else involved in the production of this novel—thank you very much.

And most of all, thank you to all the readers who picked up Volume 6 of *100-Million-Year Button*.

May we meet again in four months.

Syuichi Tsukishima